The Prince's Bride

By Lori Avocato

AmErica House
Baltimore

First printing

ISBN: 1-58851-221-5
PUBLISHED BY AMERICA HOUSE BOOK PUBLISHERS
www.publishamerica.comBaltimore
Printed in the United States of America

Dedication Page

Thanks to Sal, Mario and Greg for years of support and patience. Also, thanks to my co-writers of CTRWA and RWA online.

Chapter One

"I object!"

The familiar, polished voice sent shivers down Nola St. Clair's back–and a ripple of gasps from her wedding guests. Refusing to turn around, she looked at the chaplain whose mouth gaped open as he glared over her shoulder. She leaned near and tugged at his sleeve. "Please continue, Reverend."

"But, Ms. St. Clair, that man said he–"

"This isn't some movie of the week, Reverend Shaneborn." She forced a laugh. "No one really stops weddings in this day and age. Get past that 'let him speak now or forever part.'" She grabbed tighter onto her fiancé's arm, knowing she didn't trust herself to turn and see the unwelcome guest. There really was no need.

"Nola, what's going on? Why's he interrupting our wedding?" Rusty asked.

"Nothing's going on. Ignore him." Without missing a beat, she leaned closer to the chaplain. "Just go ahead."

"I will only object again." The rich, wonderfully European accented tone seemed to come from a distance–like a dream.

God how she wished it were. Only she'd have to call it a humdinger of a nightmare.

Rusty turned her to face him. "Maybe we should stop and see what he's talking about–"

"No!" She smiled at the man she'd loved for years, but admittedly wasn't in love with and said, "I mean...maybe he'll just leave if we ignore him." That wasn't even a probable long shot, she realized, when she noted the unwelcome guest's reflection in a picture hanging behind the reverend. The intruder kept coming closer.

Still drop-dead gorgeous.

"You can't keep ignoring me." The reflection became clearer. "I came a long distance to object. Because you know, Magnolia St. Clair, you love *me*."

"Damn," she whispered, then merely looked at Rusty and smiled at the chaplain.

A muscle twitched double-time on the poor reverend's temple. She had to think fast before the man passed out or something worse.

But before she could convince him to continue, Rusty interrupted,

5

"Magnolia?"

She blew out a breath. "What can you expect from a sixteen year old mother from Louisiana? I thank the good Lord everyday that she didn't name me 'Barbie.'"

"But I had no idea that was your real name, and he...he knew."

"Maybe it was a lucky guess. Let's get this over with–"

"Although," Rusty continued, "It sorta fits. I mean with your fair skin and light hair."

Nola groaned. By the way this wedding was going; she'd be doing a lot more groaning in the next few minutes. "Can we forget about my floral name and get on with this?"

"You know I'll do whatever you want, kiddo. But who the hell is he?" Rusty asked, then offered a few apologies to the baffled chaplain.

She knew all too well who *he* was. She shut her eyes and pictured waves, the moon's glow. Swallowing, she remembered sultry, sexy nights. Her eyes flew open. The Reverend stared. Nola's face flushed as if the minister could see inside her eyelids. The intruder stepped closer. Rusty shifted from one foot to the other. Nola groaned again, then on a sigh she said, "Del Dupre, His Royal Highness Delmar Louis Dupre."

"Royal Highness?"

"From Mirabella."

"How would a girl from the bayous of Louisiana ever meet a royal anyone?"

"Oh for crying out loud. Unfortunately, I managed," she muttered.

"Easy, Nol, you don't want to upset the baby–" Rusty touched her arm and looked at her waistline.

Her eyes widened. "Don't say anything about–" She swung around to see if Del was close enough to hear.

Big mistake.

He looked better than he did in the picture glass.

She paused. Her heart thudded. It wasn't clear if it came from waiting for him to ask what Rusty meant–or from merely looking at Del. Thankfully he remained silent. Obviously he didn't hear Rusty's comment so she turned back to the poor chaplain, who seemed frozen in time, and said, "And you, just finish the ceremony!"

He stammered a few times and managed, "But..."

Rusty interrupted, "You want me to get rid of him?" He'd been her protector for so many years, obviously he couldn't stop now.

"No! Yes! Oh God, I don't know what I'm saying–"

She could tell by the sound of his voice that Del had come further down the aisle. "Of course you are confused, *chéri*. Because you know you are making a mistake."

"I know *damn* well what I am doing!" The reverend raised an eyebrow. "Sorry, sir."

"Excuse me, Ms. St. Clair," a harried Reverend Shaneborn said. "I am not certain how to proceed." He whipped a linen hanky out of his pocket and wiped at his brow. "This has never happened to me in all my twenty-six years as a chaplain."

She let out a long sigh. "Reverend, I told you this kind of thing only happens in the movies." She envisioned Reverend Shaneborn retiring from his ministry real soon.

"Perhaps we, that is, Rusty and Nola and the visitor who has the objection, should come into my office to discuss this?"

"I would like very much to talk to Nola, alone if I may, sir," Del interrupted.

Nola refused to look at him. From the way Rusty was staring and grinning, she surmised Del must have bowed. He always did have a flair for perfect manners. Why not? He could afford to hire the best experts to teach him which fork to use or not to wash his hands in a finger bowl.

"I, uh," Reverend Shaneborn stammered, looking past Nola and Rusty. "If the entire congregation would remain seated...for at least ten...no, fifteen, make that twenty minutes, I will report to you whether we will continue with the marriage of Nola St. Clair and Rusty Breaker." He turned toward the side of the altar, stuck his hanky in his pocket, paused, took the hanky out and wiped sweat beads from his forehead before adding, "We ask your patience...and your prayers."

Nola cringed.

"Please allow me to speak to Nola, alone." Del repeated as if earlier no one had understood his accent that flowed smoother than

7

honey drizzled over a bun.

"Nola?" Rusty pulled her near. "Say the word and I'll show the guy out. What do you want to do?"

Crawl out the back door, she thought. "Russ, I appreciate you protecting me, but this isn't fair to you." She took his hand in hers, deliberately keeping herself from turning around.

"Yeah. Maybe our getting married wasn't such a good idea."

"Don't say that!" She tightened her hold. "I'm really sorry about this interruption, but you know I've always been honest about my feelings from the start."

"Well, there is that little thing about your name." He smiled.

Del cleared his throat.

Nola groaned, again.

"I'm crushed that you feel you even need to apologize. We've never led each other on or pretended we were in love–like a real couple. Well, kiddo, the ball's in your court."

"I never had my doubts about marrying you, or I wouldn't have agreed. But, I also never dreamed *this* would happen. You know I would never intentionally hurt you."

"And I would never intentionally cause a scene–if it weren't necessary," Del added.

She couldn't help herself this time. She spun around and said, "Seems we have a differing opinion of what's *necessary*." Oh geez. She shouldn't have looked at him again, let his glare capture hers. His eyes were twice as mysterious as the darkest night. Within seconds, she remembered how she used to lose her train of thought when he merely glanced toward her. As a kid she hated the dark, but since meeting Del, the night held a special enticement for her.

He grinned this time and said, "You cannot differ on true love, Nola."

She swung back around.

"This isn't all going to go away, Nol. The reverend is right. We all need to talk this thing out," Rusty said then placed a kiss on her forehead. Heat seared up her cheeks at the thought that Del stood behind watching, grinning. Damn him. Well, at least Rusty, three years her senior, didn't pat her on the head as he had been prone to do when they were kids. "I think you need to talk to him. I'll meet you in the office." He followed the reverend off the altar.

By the shuffle of footsteps, someone, most likely the maid of honor, Holly, had the thank-goodness sense to clear the guests from the chapel despite the reverend's plea they remain. Holly never did follow rules anyway. Nola faced forward, knowing Del stood several feet behind...waiting.

Silence signaled she and Del were the only two left.

She considered running through the side door, but Nola St. Clair didn't run from trouble. Hell, she'd be running her whole life if that were the case. She sucked in a breath, ignoring the skin-tight waistline of her stupid gown, turned and nearly gasped.

Del stepped forward.

She stepped back. But her disloyal body begged to go in the direction of Del's arms. His eyes held her captive, sucking her into the bottomless pools. She stifled a sigh, angry that he could still cause such a reaction. It seemed not seeing the good prince for over four months had awakened dangerous memories–ones that were getting her a bit confused. She looked away from him so she could speak without making a fool of herself. "I suppose it would be foolish of me to ask why you just ruined my wedding?"

"Nola–" He reached for her hand before she had the foresight or speed to pull away. "–I am truly sorry for interrupting like this. You know it goes against my grain to be so ill-mannered, but I'd only heard about your wedding a short time ago."

She couldn't help looking back at him. "So you high-tailed it here in your private plane."

"Jet, *chéri*." He grinned. Those dark eyes had the audacity to twinkle! He leaned, kissed her hand and smiled at the decals on her nails. "Today you chose roses."

She glanced at her hand, the skin fair and slender in the grasp of his much larger hold and forgot what she wanted to say. Tiny rose decals doted each nail, a feat that had taken her and Holly hours to accomplish. She loved variety in her nail polish–he never failed to notice.

"I have searched for a very long time and came as swiftly as I could. I had to–since I couldn't lose you."

"You can't lose...what you don't have," she said, almost a

whisper.

"Though true. You *can* recover what should be yours."

Oh God. She had no comeback for that one, damn him. So instead, she forced herself to keep looking downward. Wrong move. He tightened his hold.

Morning sunlight shone from the skylight like rays of gold to match the tawny color of his native skin. Although he had never flaunted his wealth, seeing his gold ring, the crest of the Dupre family carved in the precious metal, reminded her of his birthright–and his brother's words.

His touch made her feel like a commoner. When they'd first met, she'd never given it a second thought, but once she'd learned the truth of his heritage, his demeanor had a way of making her feel unworthy. In all honesty, she admitted, he'd never shoved his royalty down her throat. It was merely her perception. But, she had to live with herself.

And she was as common as a Louisiana bayou.

"Shall we sit? You look a bit...tired." He held his hand to the side as if she couldn't find her way to the chapel pews.

"Tired? No, Del, I'm well rested. You see, I'd gone to bed extra early last night," she raised her voice several octaves, "because today is my wedding day!"

He flinched. "Please sit."

She shut her eyes. How she loved his accent. How she hated the way it could often camouflage the real meaning of his words. Right now, however, he sounded sincere. Damn it.

"Please, Magnolia."

She glared at him and managed through a jaw tighter than the waistline of her gown, "Never, *ever* call me that."

"I apologize. But the name is appropriate. You are as beautiful as the delicate white flower of your name, *chéri*."

"And stop calling me that, too!"

"*That* I cannot do."

"Then by all means feel free to call me whatever you want. I forgot you are used to getting your own way."

The sparkle in his eyes turned to a glimmer of pain. "Not always, *chéri*, not always."

She sank onto a wooden pew. "Look, Del, as far as I'm concerned, we have nothing to discuss. I'm sorry you wasted a trip coming here. Now, if you'll be so kind as to leave, perhaps I can salvage my wedding."

He leaned against the pew, looking down. Man, he hadn't changed one iota. Damn it all but the royal Maribellan uniform, jet-black as his hair and decorated with gold braid that gave a regal look without being pretentious, hugged the guy in all the right places. And she knew very well where those places were. Nola, keep your mind out of Del's uniform and on the matter at hand.

Your wedding.

"*Chéri*, if you can tell me now that you love, more than life itself, your fiancé, I will leave—and never enter into your life again."

His words came out on a breath, warming her cheek as he leaned near. She'd barely gotten past the "*chéri*" part before what he'd asked slapped her in the face—as if he'd used more than his hot urging to knock the truth from her. She rubbed a finger across her cheek.

"After our relationship, the question remains, Nola, can you?"

She pushed to stand and eased past him, careful to avoid his gaze. "My relationship with Rusty is none of your damn business, Del. *Our* relationship—" She made the mistake of looking up. His eyes widened—pulled her in. She stood momentarily speechless.

"*Chéri?*"

"Our...'relationship—'" She glared at him. "—if that is what you chose to call it, was over four months ago." He started to say something, but she waved her hand. "I'd call it a fling, a romantic, exotic fling. Very European, I might add. But my marriage is none of your—"

"Your wedding *is* my business."

She turned away and started down the aisle. "How do you figure that?" she asked over her shoulder.

He followed close behind. "Because, *chéri*, my feelings for you have grown stronger with each day that passes as if the sun burns from the sky, adding fuel to make me miss you all the more."

Oh damn, he was good.

Those words were more potent than his hot breath on her cheek.

She spun around and grabbed onto a pew. He stood before her with a warmth radiating from the shadowy depths of his eyes. She nearly collapsed onto the seat. Instead, she straightened her shoulders, stood at attention and told him, "I made it clear four months ago, Del, when I bordered that plane back to the United States. Feelings don't matter when two people come from opposite sides of the tracks. Only in our case, it's opposite sides of the world. It's millenniums away. It's black and white. It's...you and I."

"But–"

"Please–don't." She turned to walk back to the reverend's office.

"Nola–" he whispered, "–if you give me more time."

"Time won't change a thing. I'm going to talk to Rusty to see if we can salvage our wedding." She took a step.

"You may be able to save your wedding day, Nola, but what of your marriage?"

She paused, turned. "*That*, Your Highness, is none of your concern." Before he could counter, she hurried up the altar steps and through the door, hoping against hope that Rusty was still in Reverend Shaneborn's office.

She hesitated in the hallway at the sound of voices behind the office door. Rusty hadn't left yet. She could always count on her dear friend. She knocked and followed the chaplain's invitation to come in. When she opened the door, Rusty sprang from his seat.

"Kiddo, are you all right?"

"Fine, Rus."

"What about him?" He nodded in Del's direction.

"Forget him. He'll be leaving." She pushed Rusty to the side. "We can continue–if you still want to marry me."

He took her into his arms. "Like I said, whatever you want." The warmth she'd felt earlier from Del now prickled like tiny needles under her skin. This was ridiculous. She loved Rusty–but his touch didn't make her want to melt into a puddle.

"My relationship with Del was over months ago. He's not in the picture, nor will he ever be "

"But, Nol, he's the father of your baby."

She kicked the door shut. "I never said that!" Without a thought, she rubbed at her waistline, certain the slight bulge had grown since this morning.

Rusty covered her hand with his. "You didn't have to."

"You assumed," she whispered.

Rusty nodded.

"Don't ever assume things where I am concerned. It will cause problems. I'm not exactly predictable. You've known that for years."

He kissed her on the forehead. "Yeah, but I figured there was still hope." They chuckled.

"Thanks for being you, trying to lighten the mood."

"Sorry I can't do more–like make the right decision for you."

Rusty took her into his arms and pulled her close. Not as a lover, more a dear friend. "Level with yourself. Do you love him, kiddo?"

"I–" Rusty held her a few minutes. "Of course not."

"Then, let's get hitched."

She should be apologizing to him, but she couldn't summon the words. If she did, they'd come in a flood of tears and Nola St. Clair didn't allow herself to cry. She'd shed the tears of a lifetime at age seven and since had grown too tough to let emotion take control of her actions. Easing free of Rusty's hold, she kissed him on the cheek and looked at the chaplain. "Is it too late to continue?"

He cleared his throat and gave her a fatherly nod. "You may–" He wiped at his forehead, sans hanky. "If you are certain."

"I...am."

Rusty walked her to the door. He would make a wonderful, caring father, she told herself.

She *needed* to marry him today.

When Rusty opened the door, Del stood in the doorway. "Excuse me." Rusty tried to ease past, but Nola noticed he seemed reluctant to touch Del. That aura of nobility made one hesitate in his presence. Or, more than likely, Rusty was having a dickens of a time not popping Del one for ruining her day.

Del stepped forward and looked at Nola. "You are certain?"

She nodded.

"Then may I stay to celebrate your special day with you?"

"I'd rather you–"

"Sure, your highness," Rusty interrupted. "That's the least we can do, kiddo."

Nola moved past Del. "Sit in back, and keep your mouth shut."

Nola took her place next to Rusty at the altar. Numbness had settled in the pit of her stomach. Good thing, or else she might not be able to remain. Reluctantly, she looked over her shoulder.

The wedding guests filtered back to their seats, no doubt wondering what the heck was going on. She turned toward Holly and forced a smile. Despite Nola's best efforts, she could see the questions in her friend's eyes. She mouthed, "Keep quiet," to Holly and yanked her glare toward the seats now full on Rusty's side of the church. He had been adopted into the Breaker family as a teen–the lucky son of a gun, she'd always told him–so he had two brothers and a sister to attend today.

The bride's side, however, barely filled a fourth of the pews. Oh, she had friends here, but when your immediate family consisted of a mother's name on your birth certificate, it left the pews a bit sparse.

Seated in the last one, because of the rows of empty seats in front of him, Del stood out. Or maybe, she admitted, his regal presence set him off from the rest. Nola sucked in a breath as if that would increase her courage then turned toward the reverend.

He seemed to have aged since the ceremony had begun.

Reverend Shaneborn cleared his throat and proceeded in a fog of words. Nola watched Rusty's mouth move, but she couldn't hear a thing. His eyes held no warmth, no depth to suck her into him. She shouldn't be paying attention to things like that right now, but, as if Del's presence had heightened her emotions, she noticed everything.

Rusty had an annoying habit of swallowing between every third or fourth word. Normally she wouldn't care–hell, she'd teased him about it a million times when they were kids. Today, his eyes seemed to bore into her, like a laser of ice. Man, she was in bad shape. Lasers produced heat, but the affect Rusty's look had on her could only be described as–cold. The love between them was not what marriages were made of. She felt like a liar. A fake, a fraud. A fraud that didn't want to hurt someone like Rusty.

"I do," Rusty said.

"You can't," she interrupted.

Chapter Two

The reverend's hand began to shake as if he sensed this was going to be a ceremony he would never forget. Nola felt horrible, but she still hoped he wouldn't yank out his hanky again. The thing had to be soaked.

"You can't marry me, Rusty. I'm not right for you and no matter how much we say it will work–" She took Rusty's hand into hers.

"It won't," he finished.

"Right." She held his hand to her cheek and said, "I am so sorry."

Rusty smiled and kissed her cheek. "Don't be, Nol. I think I knew all along that this wasn't right. Not that I don't love you, I do. But you know it's special, but not what marriages are made of. I'm glad you had the nerve to stop it before we were both sorry. Guess the old prince did us a favor."

"One could look at it that way."

"Hey, now I can chase after that skirt in Accounting."

She laughed and poked him in the side. "We both deserve true love." She kissed him on the cheek.

The chaplain leaned forward. "We're not going through with this. Are we?"

"No," Nola and Rusty said together. She was glad to see there was no pain in Rusty's eyes. She couldn't bear to hurt someone who had been willing to offer her so much.

Only all for the wrong reasons.

She turned toward the guests who seemed ready to take flight to the outdoors once again. "Okay, as you heard, the wedding is cancelled. But since the reception is all paid for, and you know how I can't stand to waste money, let's all head there to celebrate Rusty's and my un-wedding!" Thank goodness a hearty chuckle came from Rusty, easing the guilt Nola felt. She should have known they were both on the same wavelengths and could trust that he'd agree, but after the 'incident' with Del, her thoughts were still in turmoil.

"Want me to drive you over, kiddo?" Rusty asked.

"No. I want a few minutes alone. I'll walk."

"Sure." Rusty instructed the guests on how to get to the reception hall down the street amid joking about being jilted. Laughter mingled along with the wedding music as everyone filed out of the chapel.

Del remained seated.

Holly leaned toward Nola. "Want moral support, kid?"

"No. Thanks anyway."

In a whisper Holly said, "But you know how he makes you crazy. I mean, when you'd gotten back from Mirabella, you'd told me how you couldn't think clearly around him."

Nola sighed. "Yeah, I know. But now I have someone else to consider, so nothing is going to muddy the waters of my brain. That is...*he* is not going to even though his showing up here today has my mind cloudier than the muddy Mississippi."

Holly hesitated. "Okay. You know yourself, kid. Rusty would have been a good catch, but I can see you have someone else on the line."

"Puleez, Hol. Go make sure everyone has fun at the reception. I'll be right over." Nola watched Holly walk down the aisle, stop and give a friendly handshake to Del. Without a word between them, he kissed Holly's hand and although it was a gesture of friendship, Nola touched her face, knowing how those lips felt.

Through the open door she saw the ushers who were to hold a canopy of flowers for the bride and groom to walk under. Thank goodness they weren't magnolias.

As Holly and Rusty disappeared down the steps, Nola lifted her gown and sat on the top step of the altar. "So, what the hell are you doing in the States anyway?"

He remained at a safe distance in his seat and said, "Business."

"How convenient."

"My Dallas office scheduled it months ago, Nola. However, I am forever grateful that I was in America to hear about your wedding. And I won't deny I rushed here today to–"

"Don't rub it in."

"I'm not like that."

"I didn't hear any hesitation in your 'I object.'"

"Because there wasn't any."

He'd made her heart flutter when she would have preferred to skip that particular beat. Well, that one backfired, she thought.

He ran his gaze around the chapel. "I won't lie, Nola. I'm glad I came today. You will thank me someday–"

16

She sighed. "Gloating isn't becoming of a future ruler."

"I'm not gloating."

She leaned forward in a mocking stare. "Oh no, you are the epitome of remorse."

"You know that I feel terrible for what happened here, but it needed to be stopped–before it was too late."

She yanked up her gown, revealing the stupid blue garter Holly had insisted she wear. While it would have been wasted on Rusty, Del's gaze locked onto it, searing into her skin. She made a mental note to shoot Holly. First that damn backless dress, now this. "Where are you staying?" She pulled her dress over her knees.

"I've taken a small place on a monthly basis–in the Hillside Arms."

Oh great neighbors, she thought. "Right across the courtyard from me. Talk about bad luck–" She paused and glared at him. "Or damn good research."

"I did my research."

"Maybe I can sublet and become a hermit in the mountains." He leaned back, hands clasped behind his head with a cocky smile on his face. This is not good, she thought on a heavy sigh.

"So, how long have you been here, anyway?" Thank goodness she'd gotten a good night's sleep or the way she felt right now, she would pass out. Emotion–and dealing with Del–was exhausting.

"I only arrived a few hours ago."

"And high-tailed it over to ruin my wedding."

"Stop, not ruin." He smiled. "I didn't even take time for breakfast, and you know that is my favorite meal of the day."

She curled her lip. "I guess since you have to eat, you can stop by the reception–for a quick bite, that is." She yanked at the wedding gown and started down the aisle. "You probably had it all planned out that you would anyway."

"Thank you, *chéri*." Del smiled to himself at Nola's reaction. She looked like an adorable child. Rosy cheeks like strawberries bathed in rich heavy cream. Pale golden hair gave cognizance to her floral namesake and spilled out beneath the yellow rose crown she wore. Best of all, though, he loved to see the way her mouth scrunched up to one side when he called her "*chéri*." He didn't use the term to intentionally anger her, but any reaction right now was appreciated.

One thing he couldn't take from Nola was being ignored.

Despite being hounded by the press and living his fishbowl-type lifestyle, he still knew all too well how being ignored felt. And it was that very thought, he reminded himself, that had him wishing on a daily basis that he'd been born into any other family besides the Royal Dupres.

Nola paused at the end of the aisle. "I'm guessing you have your own means of transportation?"

"I drove the car I keep in Dallas."

She nodded and headed out the door. A silver Porsche sat in the parking lot. No one she had invited drove a car like that. From the corner of her eye, she watched Del coming toward the parking lot headed for the car. He opened the door and sank into the driver's seat. She curled her lip and picked up her pace.

Del drove out of the lot. Halfway down the street, Nola, wedding gown hiked up to her knees and floral headdress askew, trudged on. Maybe he imagined it, but it looked as if steam poured out of her ears. Apparently no one had seen fit to wait for the un-bride. He pulled up and opened his window. "Excuse me, *chéri*, is it a right or a left to the reception hall?"

"Real men don't ask for directions." She kept on walking.

Del chuckled and drove along, although if she kept up her pace, he'd get a ticket for speeding. "Wasn't it you who had accused me of not being a real man before? I believe you used the term "royal pain in the–"

"Ascot. Yeah, I said that. But don't go by me. Princes obviously get under my skin." She stumbled and caught her balance.

"Do you know many princes?" How he'd like to run his hands across that skin he got under, knowing how soft, how warm and velvety it felt, but instead, he forced his mind on the road.

She glared at him, the heels of her shoes scuffing along the sidewalk. "No. And I'm certain that is a blessing."

"Nola, do you want a ride?"

She stopped, turned and walked toward his car. "The last thing I want today is a ride from you." Nevertheless, she flopped into the passenger seat, flipped off her shoes and said, "Whoever invented heels should be shot. No, better yet he should be forced to wear them–for hours."

"He?"

"No female would come up with such a stupid idea for a fellow woman."

Del chuckled and pulled out onto the road leading to the reception hall.

Beep. Beep.

Nola turned and curled her lip. "What now? You're planning to blow us up so no other man can have me?"

Del shook his head, then lifted the face of his watch and said, "Yes, Henri?"

Nola leaned near. "Oh man, is that you, Henri Bernard, in that watch?"

A chuckle came across followed by the voice of Del's trusted assistant, "Hello, *Mademoiselle* Nola. How are you?"

She nearly pulled Del's arm from the steering wheel. "Can you see me?"

"*Oui, Mademoiselle.*"

"Cool! A little TV set on a wrist. You're so...tiny."

"Uh, only on the screen."

She yanked Del's wrist as she laughed.

He pulled into a nearby parking lot and shut off the engine before Nola had them diverted into a lane of traffic. "He can see you, *chéri.*"

"What will you Mirabellans think of next? Such a tiny country filled with so many 'techno geeks.' Oh, I didn't mean you were a geek, Hank."

Henri chuckled. Del thought the color of the screen might need adjusting until he remembered his assistant always blushed when Nola became so familiar. Poor Henri wasn't raised with such candor.

"You know we are proud to be a major exporter in technology, *Mademoiselle* Nola."

Del felt his eyebrows raise and whispered to Nola. "Quick. Change the subject before Henri spiels off the staggering statistics of my country's wealth."

Nola glared at him and pulled the watch closer to ask, "How've you been, Hank?"

"Fine. And yourself?"

She pulled at Del's arm again until the watch aimed in her direction. "I'm wearing white, Hank, and you know that's not my color with this pale skin. I'm nearly invisible. And to top it off, it's a white wedding gown."

Del flinched. Henri cleared his throat. "I'm guessing congratulations are in order?"

Nola shoved Del's arm to the side. "Only for your Royal Highness who managed to ruin my wedding."

"Yes...er...oh my. Perhaps this is not a good time, Your Highness?"

Del looked at Henri and said, "Is the matter pressing?"

"It's your father..."

Del pulled his wrist from Nola's hold. "What's wrong? Is he all right? Did he get—"

"He is fine, sir. He never left the palace. But, uh, it seems he over-ordered a few supplies for the building of the new center."

"So?"

"By four times," Henri finished.

"Damn. Can't you send them back?"

"We've tried, but he insists we need them."

Del blew out a breath and ignored Nola's raised eyebrows. "Store them. If there is nothing else, I'll call you later. Oh, Henri, Damien is not to know about this."

Nola winced at the mention of Del's brother and leaned toward the watch. "Bye, Hank."

Henri sputtered a goodbye before the screen went blank. Del shoved the car into drive and headed out of the parking lot. "Poor Henri is probably downing a pint of my finest Scotch right now. You have that affect on the man." They stopped at a red light.

"He's a darling, and you know he doesn't drink," she said lightly.

A look of concern covered her eyes. How he loved that shade of blue, so like the sea near the palace.

She grew serious. "Is everything all right back home?"

"Fine." He couldn't go into any detail with Nola. Not that he didn't trust her, but his allegiance to his country had to prevail over

20

everything right now—not to mention that the problem touched him too personally. The future of Mirabella might someday be in his hands—and how he hated that.

But as much as he hated that, he'd hate it more if it ended up in Damien's.

Nola leaned back. He suspected—or at least hoped—she was thinking of the days they'd spent in his homeland after he'd met her in France.

His life had never been the same.

So clearly he remembered dancing with Nola on the porch overlooking the moonlit beach. Finding the slightest excuse to toast a sip of champagne as if it were water. Making love. Although only once, it had been the best of his entire life. How he wanted more, wanted to please her again. He'd spent their final days together trying to convince her of how he felt—and that she could belong there, be part of his country.

Now he'd come halfway across the world to recapture those days.

Nola broke into his daydreaming. "Good. I'm glad everything is all right in your home. Give my regards to your parents the next time your watch rings."

"I shall."

He smiled sadly. Would his father remember Nola, the woman who had spent months in their palace, making him laugh? The queen, on the other hand, would probably like to forget the spirited American who turned the royal household upside down in that short time.

"By the way," Nola asked, "how does that thing work?"

Del glanced at his watch. "Similar to a beeper, but more sophisticated since we are able to see each other. This one is portable as you can see, but I also have a much larger screen set up wherever I stay."

"Wow. Hank can call you anytime?"

Del chuckled. "Henri values his job and knows enough to check the time here in America before he calls me. Unless it is an emergency, of course."

"Of course," she whispered. She pointed toward the left. "You can let me off here."

He looked at her. The excitement of seeing Henri had faded, overtaken by a solemn look.

"Less walking on these blasted shoes," she said, but he knew she didn't want to be seen coming in with him.

"Oh gosh, kid, he looks so...so divine, heavenly, swarthy, like some European god. You never told me how wonderful–"

Nola shoved her hand over Holly's mouth. "Shut up, Hol, I saw him today, too. He's the reason this finger is naked. Remember?" She wiggled her ring finger in front of her friend's face.

Holly gave an annoying but-he's-still-so-gorgeous sigh. "You've got to admit, it's for the best."

"I don't have to admit anything. I'm known for my obscurity." She gathered up the crinoline folds of her gown and pulled. The tearing of fabric gave a finality to the day, and caused a look of horror on Holly's face. "You should be in *B* movies, Hol. Here, pull."

"But, that dress is...was gorgeous."

"Pull!" Nola gave another yank. "I have to get out of this thing–this reminder." When the last layer landed on the ladies' room floor, Nola looked at herself in the mirror. "Maybe I should design fashion instead of doing OR nursing?" The remainder, a snug fitting silken white slip of a dress, looked damn good.

"Wow. Not bad. Maybe you should. It hugs you in all the right places." Holly leaned nearer. "You don't even show yet."

"Thank goodness my waistline is holding its own." Nola turned to make sure. "You're not just saying that...because–"

"He'll never guess, but when are you going to tell him?"

"Never. And don't you breathe a word–"

A pained look replaced the B star quality of Holly's face. Maybe she'd be better in a drama. "You know I never would, Nola."

Nola sighed, and flopped into the nearest seat. "I'm sorry, Hol. I know you wouldn't." With legs outstretched, she slumped further down.

"For the life of me, I can't figure out why you want to keep his baby a secret." Holly joined her, sinking into a nearby sofa.

"It would never work. We come from two different worlds–"

"Nola, when are you going to let your past go?"

"I'd like to...but I can't. And I don't need to be reminded of it on a daily basis."

"I can't believe Del would–"

"No..." She sighed. "He wouldn't. But his brother Damien and the queen are a different matter."

"They said something?"

"She never had to. Damien got me alone one night and made it quite clear that I would be the downfall of Del's reign."

"The bas–"

"He was right, Holly."

Holly frowned. "I don't agree, but you still need to forget the past. You, Rusty and I have turned out fab." She grinned. Nola looked at her, and they laughed. Holly took Nola's hand. "You should tell Del about his child."

Nola sighed, and thought of how her friend was asking the impossible. "It just would not be fair to Del or–" She ran her hand across her silk-covered abdomen. "Him or her."

"I can't wait to find out." Holly chewed a nail, something that obviously helped her think.

"Stop doing that! Biting nails is tantamount to sacrilege."

Holly laughed. "I know. I know. No one takes as much care of their nails as you. It comes from you secluding yourself in your room as a kid and painting them hideous colors." Holly shook her head. "It's not fair what adults can do to kids."

She placed a hand on Nola's shoulder. "Getting back to the here and now. Your nails are always gorgeous now, by the way. Nol, you're so levelheaded–high-spirited, sure, but probably the most cautious person I know. I've never been able to understand how you got pregnant. I know it's none of my business, and don't feel shy about telling me to shut up–"

"Faulty condom."

"Oh gosh, what are the odds?"

"Apparently better than winning the lotto. I may be levelheaded as you say–but Lord knows, I've never, *ever* been lucky."

"You don't allow yourself to be, Nol."

She looked at her friend; "Things are not always in my control. Look what happened the first time I ventured out of town."

Holly touched her arm. "Nol, I know how you fought your boss about taking that assignment to Mirabella, but you know, it's not like you'll fall madly in love with a prince every time you leave town. You need to leave the security of–"

"I don't plan on leaving again. I was fine until that trip. The flight to Europe had my heart racing continuously. Hol, the minute we drove out of town to the airport, I felt panic. Then, to top off my fears of straying from home–I fell hard for Del–"

"That's obvious, to me at least. Of course, I know you like a sister, not to mention the fact that you'd told me how wonderful it was when you two first met. Besides, kid, I know you don't jump into bed with just anyone."

"If I knew he was a prince..." She pushed herself to stand. "I have to eat or I'll puke."

Holly laughed. "That's my Nola!" She followed Nola to the door and added, "Well, I still think it's the best thing that's ever happened to you. Having him stop your wedding that is. I mean, Nol, it's like a fairytale. Handsome prince rushes in to save damsel in distress." Nola though she heard Holly purr as she walked out the door.

"It isn't like he slew some dragon for me, for crying out loud. All he did was stop me from marrying Rusty."

"Whom you don't love, at least not in *that* way."

Nola glared at her well meaning, though utterly annoying best friend. "Remember that old song, 'What's Love Got To Do With It?'"

"Oh, Nola, love has *everything* to do with it. And, you will start believing in love when you're swept off your feet by the real thing... a real man, that is. And Del sure looks real with a capital *R*." The letter rolled off her tongue.

Nola snorted.

Holly grabbed her hand and said, "Don't let years of hurting cause you more pain."

Nola slipped her hand away. "Thanks for your concern, Hol, although I could argue with your romantic logic until I'm blue in the face, but the lack of oxygen couldn't be good for you know who." She patted her stomach. "I really have to eat something."

Holly gave her a nudge. "Go. Hurry. Eat."

Nola made her way toward the buffet table. Seems the closer she got, the aroma of food had her stomach doing back-flips. *Don't get sick. Don't get sick.* She ran her latest mantra through her thoughts as she forked a roll. *Dry food is good for you. Dry food goes down like chalk but stays down, hopefully. Dry food is...damn, it's gonna be impossible to get down with the way I feel.*

"Butter, *chéri?*"

Greasy, rich, greasy, butter. Nola's stomach lurched. Before she could remedy the confused look on Del's face, she shoved her plate at him and ran.

"*Chéri?*"

Don't follow me, she prayed as she made her way into the ladies' room just in time.

Holly was fast on her heels. "Are you all right, kid?" She paused outside the door. "Oh no, he's going to guess, Nola!"

"Oh sure–" She came out of the stall to wash her face. "It's a given that any female who looses it is pregnant?"

"No, but–"

"We only made love once. He can't be that smart to put two and a million together."

"Well, no. But he was smart enough to ferret you out in time to stop your wedding."

"Yeah, yeah." Splashes of cold water revived her and calmed her stomach. She splashed more. "Granted, he is smart. A whiz at technology, a damn good businessman, and hell of a good looker, Holly. But he is *not* a mind reader. At least I hope not." She gave her friend a hug, looked in the mirror and groaned.

"Here. Use my lipstick." Holly shoved her purse toward Nola. "Put some on your cheeks, too. I didn't bring my blush."

Nola leaned closer to the mirror. "I need more than lipstick on my cheeks."

"You look beautiful, even after puking, kid."

"You're a great friend, and a top-notch liar." She handed Holly her purse, gave her a quick hug, turned and headed out.

Del waited in the hallway. "Are you all right?"

"Fine now, but don't offer me...that stuff again. Ever." He looked at her with one raised eyebrow as if he could not only see into her head, but her soul as well. Her heart flipped faster than her stomach had before. Maybe swarthy Mirabellans *are* mind readers, she thought. "A touch of lactose intolerance," she said.

"Excuse me?"

"My running off like that." She sighed. "Look, it's just that I hadn't eaten all day. My blood sugar must have plummeted."

"Go sit down. I'll get you a plate of food." He stepped forward and pressed a hand into her back. A hot hand.

"You don't know–" Del's fingers moved over the backless section of her dress. Nola wondered why the reception manager was so stingy with the air conditioning. You could fry an egg on the dance floor in this...heat. She made a mental note to complain. She wiggled from his touch and said, "I can stand fine, get my own food, and don't need your help. You don't know what I want to eat anyway." He dropped his hand, took a step back, and thank goodness, the temperature cooled. She decided not to bother with her complaint.

"Your beautiful gown–"

"I was hot." She pushed past him and headed toward the buffet table, telling herself that the food smelled delicious and that his laser glare was not following her. When she turned to peek over her shoulder, Del remained, leaning against the wall, watching. Damn, what were those adjectives Holly had used? Divine, heavenly, and what was it? Oh, yeah, swarthy like some European god. Nola shoved a roll into her mouth and bit off a huge chunk.

Holly *was* smart about some things.

"Nola? Can I get you anything?" Rusty asked, coming up from behind. The temperature dropped considerably.

She wondered why men thought her incapable of foraging for her own food, then reminded herself they were gentlemen. It was a toss up as to who was more polite with Del representing Mirabella, and Rusty the good old U.S.A. They were condescendingly chauvinistic in her opinion.

As a kid in Louisiana, she'd dreamed of men who waited on women instead of visa versa. But in the homes she grew up in, that practice didn't exist. Too often it felt like culture shock when someone opened her car door, or offered to get her food.

With a mouthful, she managed, "No thanks, Rusty, I'm fine." Not use to being pampered, she wasn't certain she could trust the sincerity of that action from anyone.

Or at least, she thought as Del's dark glare burned into her, not from any man.

Especially princes.

Chapter Three

Nola paused a moment to look at Del. Well, she actually had no choice since he remained perched against the wall, watching her. It only seemed fair and sensible to stare back. Besides, if she dropped a fork he'd probably be at her feet in a flash–and she wanted to be ready for him. It wasn't as if he gave her the creeps staring at her like some stalker–that she could deal with. No, it was more those blasted sensual eyes made her already weak knees weaker. Her stomach growled, sending a warning of hunger and wave of nausea all at once.

Nausea is good. Nausea is good. She chose to believe it meant her hormone levels were high. Somehow, knowing it was good for the baby made the awful sensation more tolerable. Holly says nausea is good, she reminded herself again when she felt her insides jiggle. Seems mantras occupied her thoughts every day lately. The best part of repeating these mantras, she thought, was the warmth of maternal love that grew deep inside–something so very new to her and so wonderful.

Rusty'd excused himself to go find a new "skirt" to dance with. Nola looked down at her plate. She had to eat, but what? Her mouth felt drier than when the dentist stuck that sucking thing into it. Running her tongue across her teeth, she told herself she needed protein. Since meat had been rationed most places she lived as a kid, it had never held much interest for her. Lately she'd gone the carnivorous route, though, because her OB doctor had said she needed a lot of protein. Besides, she couldn't fathom eating dozens of eggs or bricks of cheese. Funny, she'd eat a side of beef right now if it would insure a healthy baby.

"You need to sit, *chéri.*"

Nola's head flew up while an olive danced off her plate, landing on Del's expensive looking leather shoes. She glared at the fool thing sitting on top of the black leather, debating what to do. No way did she want to touch any part of him, even his stupid shoe. Maybe it would roll off, and she'd kick it under the table.

When she looked up, a twinkle in his eyes said he knew she hesitated, knew the kind of affect he had on her. *Damn him.* Hopefully he really couldn't read minds. His glance shifted from the olive to her plate. There was no way she wanted to explain why she

29

was eating red meat or so much food in general for that matter. "Sorry about the shoe." The olive hadn't budged. Oh hell, she thought, what is he going to do in such a public place? Ravish me? So she bent to pick it up, but before she made it all the way down, Del took her arm, lifting her up.

"Allow me."

She wasn't about to argue since her nausea had joined forces with a new ailment. Dizziness. If she didn't bring her darn blood sugar level up, they'd be scraping her off Del's shoe. "Okay. I'm going to sit down."

Before he could say a word, she eased through the crowd to an empty table. Rusty had seated himself at the head table, but she felt foolish sitting there, the center of attraction, when she really had nothing to celebrate. An un-wedding wasn't exactly something to raise the roof over. Of course, looking at Rusty right now and not feeling the slightest titillation, maybe it really was cause to celebrate. She smiled to herself when two female guests joined him.

"Feel better now?" Del asked.

She looked up. He'd removed his jacket. All that was left was a starched white shirt with sleeves pushed above his elbows. Titillation, on the other hand, was a mild term to use for the jittery, mind-scrambling feelings that seeing the good prince's pecs produced. With a tug to her wandering brain, Nola reminded herself to eat and shoved a carrot dripping in salsa into her mouth. She followed that with a slice of roast beef, rolled up to get the most into her mouth at once. Man, she really was starving. Her mind started to clear, the dizziness lifted, and the grumbles from her stomach quieted. "Um. I'm fine. Go ahead."

"Where?" Del asked, pulling the back of the nearest chair away from the table.

Anywhere but here, she thought. "You must have somewhere to go. Some business to take care of." Taking another bite of roast beef, she muttered, "Call someone on your watch."

Del sat and chuckled. "No business on Saturday, *chéri*, and Henri is fast asleep right now since it is past his bedtime in Mirabella. You know he would verbally throttle me for waking him. He is not prone to chats during the night."

She couldn't help but laugh. "You're right about that. He's a bit of a nervous-Nelly."

"What is this nervous-Nelly?"

She looked at him over her salami, which she'd rolled up beneath a piece of camouflage provolone. "Someone who worries too much."

"Ah," he said, then laughed. "True enough. Henri is worse than a mother chicken."

"Hen. Worse than a mother hen, although chicken mothers may very well worry about their young, too." She bit her salami-provolone roll.

"That is if chickens are mothers. Perhaps they only lay eggs we eat. Maybe hens produce the young?" he said, then laughed.

"We'll have to research–" We'll? What the heck was she talking about? Chickens, hens, and spending time researching with Del? "Anyway, Henri is adorable," she said to get the conversation back on track. Besides, she didn't like the direction of that chicken/hen stuff. Too close to mothers and babies.

Del lifted her napkin from her lap and touched at her chin. "Henri is dedicated. I could not function without him."

When she looked at the napkin in his hand, she said, "What the hell are you doing?"

"Salsa," he whispered and unfortunately wiped again. If she thought the room was warm before, it'd become downright hot now–and it wasn't from the salsa.

Gently she eased her chin from the napkin. "Guess you can dress me up, but can't take me out." She laughed, trying to get her focus from his touch to anything else in the world, even a stupid cliché.

But her plan backfired when Del leaned disturbingly near and said, "I would take you out no matter what you were dressed in." His fool eyes twinkled as he whispered, "Even if you wore *nothing*."

She tried to move away, but her traitorous body planted itself within breathing distance of him.

"By the way, I like what you did to your gown."

He turned his glare downward, letting it slide across the silk, barely hiding her figure. He hesitated, she thought, when it came to her waistline. Oh God was she starting to show? It was a crazy fear since she'd seen herself in the ladies' room mirror only minutes ago.

31

But by the way he looked at her, she wouldn't be surprised if he could see right into her womb to see their baby sucking its thumb.

Well, if he mentioned anything, she'd blame the bulge on the amount of food she'd just devoured. She looked at her empty plate and wondered if there was anymore salami left. "That crinoline stuff was much too stiff for my taste."

"Why did you buy it, then?"

"Blame it on Holly."

"Blame what on me?" Holly asked from behind.

"My wedding gown." Nola shoved the chair next to her away from the table. At least Holly would be a buffer. "Sit."

"Thanks, no. I'm going to—"

Nola yanked at her arm. "Sit. I insist. You look tired, Hol."

Holly, not very tactfully in fact, looked at Del. "Oh, yeah. I am a bit...warm."

"Tired," Nola correct and raised her eyes. Maybe this wasn't such a good idea.

Del smiled and took Holly's hand. Nola guessed he wasn't about to read her palm, although, lately it seemed he may have a knack for that sort of thing. True to form, he leaned and kissed Holly's hand. Nola looked at the ceiling in disgust. Holly sighed. You'd think Del was *her* lover. Nola pulled her head and her mind back to reality. Where'd *that* come from? Not that she didn't trust her friend, but a niggling of jealousy had replaced the disgust. She'd rather have the disgust back, she thought. Jealousy was not her style.

Besides, Nola St. Clair, he's not *your* lover either.

"We have not been officially introduced," Del said.

"Hm?" Nola managed as Holly merely batted her eyelashes at the prince. Oh man, he's sucking her in with his royal web. "Sorry. Holly Carmichael, His Royal Highness Del Dupre."

"Charmed," Del said.

"We met briefly in the chapel, but this beats a quickie like that."

Holly took her hand back, thank goodness, but glared at it as if he'd left some kind of sexual imprint on her skin. Man, Hol, get a grip, Nola thought—even though it's tough to do where Del was concerned. "Well, now that the formalities are over with, what are you up to, Holly?"

"Why...I..." She giggled. Nola cringed. "I actually forgot why I came over here." As if it were Nola's fault for the memory loss, Holly glared at her. "You pulled me down, and I forgot."

Nola shook her head. "Nice to have you join us, anyway," she said, although she'd like to shake some sense into her mesmerized friend. How could one man make an intelligent woman–and Holly was one of the smartest nurses in OB–make such a fool of herself? Okay, he was more charming in a European sort of way than any man here, any doctor at St. Lucinda's Hospital where they worked–okay, in the world, but Holly's reaction and hers, too, she admitted, was based on the novelty of Del's behavior–nothing else.

"So what brings you to an out-of-the-way-place like Soledad?" Holly asked.

Nola kicked her friend under that table.

"Ouch! Oh, I mean, other than...well, you know–"

Del gave Holly a knowing smile and bailed her out by saying, "My most important mission was accomplished this morning."

Nola curled her lips.

"But I do have other business here, too."

"How convenient," Nola added.

"Yeah, that is," concurred Holly as if she hadn't caught on that Del planned to be here to stop Nola's wedding. Nola scrutinized her friend. Maybe she wasn't the smartest OB nurse, come to think of it.

"It did work out rather nicely. My country, although small, is a major manufacturer in microscopic equipment. Our technology is used in many operating rooms including state of the art lasers."

Nola groaned, knowing she couldn't get away from Del once she went back to work on Monday. Obviously she would cancel her vacation since she wasn't going on any honeymoon with Rusty, so she'd have to deal with Del's "convenient business" once she went back to work. The thought of keeping the vacation and hiding out in her apartment tempted her.

Hell, no way would she waste a week's vacation trying to avoid him.

"Neat country you come from," Holly said. She went on like some fool saying, "So, your company has a contract with St. Lucinda's for OR equipment?"

"We have, along with other technology. I will be making the rounds to a few other hospitals while I am stateside."

Nola sat forward. "When?" Maybe she wouldn't have to sidestep him for long.

He looked at her as if he knew she was eager for him to leave. Well of course he knew that, she'd made it clear this morning in the chapel. Then again, she thought, she'd made it clear four months ago when she stepped on the plane in Mirabella.

Obviously the Royal Intruder couldn't take a hint.

"Depends on how long it takes here."

A chill chased up Nola's back. It wasn't from the damn backless dress. She guessed Del wasn't talking OR equipment any longer.

"However, I cannot leave my country for too long," he added. Before Nola could mumble, "Good," he asked, "what is it you do here, Holly?"

"I'm a nurse, like Nola."

"Operating room?"

"Oh, no. Too boring for me, sorry, Nol."

Nola nodded, not caring if Holly insulted her job, her name, her looks, heck, her family if she had one. "No, I work in Obstetrics. The clinic part, not Labor and Delivery, although nothing in the world is going to keep me out of the delivery room when– Ouch!"

Nola stood. She must have left a gigantic bruise on Holly's leg with her shoe, but before she could think of what else to do or say, Holly obviously got the idea.

"When...they deliver the triplets that one of the patients is pregnant with. In...April," she added apparently an afterthought.

"June, you mean, Hol," Nola said, since today was May fifteenth.

Holly managed a laugh. "How silly. I meant June. It's just that I was thinking–"

Nola grabbed her arm, knowing Holly was doing way too much thinking. "I've got a craving for sugar. Butter creme frosting roses, red ones to be exact."

Holly's eyes widened, but even Nola didn't think Del was that clairvoyant enough to associate a sweet-tooth craving with pregnancy. "Let's go get a slab of cake."

Del stood and started to bow.

Nola pushed past him, saying, "We'll bring you back some." She made up a fast prayer that he'd get the hint and stay put. This wasn't the first time she wished she'd been raised with a formal religion so she'd know a prayer or two when she needed one. But from what she remembered of her mother, she wasn't exactly a pious individual.

Once out of Del's earshot, Nola shook Holly's arm. "You almost told him!"

Genuine worry filled Holly's eyes. "Oh Lord, Nola. I didn't mean to–" Holly sniffled.

"I know, Hol." She patted her arm.

"It almost slipped out. One, cause I'm so excited for you. And two, my mind didn't seem to be functioning right for some reason."

"Del."

"What?"

"Del." Nola hugged her. "I certainly understand and don't worry. He has some strange power over women."

A dreamy look replaced the worry in Holly's eyes. "Magical."

Nola shut her eyes and felt Del's lips on hers. It had been months, but the feeling returned as if it were only moments ago that he'd kissed her. Against her better judgment, she agreed, "It is magic." Suddenly she thought even magic couldn't help her now. Her mind snapped to attention. She pulled Holly near. "Magic, smagic. He *can't* find out."

"All right." Holly leaned near, looking sympathetic. "I'll be careful, Nol, but I'm more confused than ever as to why you don't want your baby's father to be a prince?"

"We've been through that, Hol. Right now I need to start looking for a replacement for Rusty."

Holly groaned. "Don't tell me you're going to try to marry someone else?"

"My baby–"

"I know, Nol. You think your baby needs a father. But maybe you're letting your loss as a kid mix up your mind a bit."

Nola couldn't be angry with her friend. They had been too close all these years, and Holly and Rusty were the only people who knew her past. "I know how it feels to be teased, Hol."

"Your situation was different, kid. No way are you going to be like your mother."

"No, I'm not. But those early years have scarred me–I admit that much."

"Then learn from it, but don't let it ruin you."

Holly meant well. Nola didn't dispute what she said. Of course her past had affected her life–whose didn't? "My baby is going to have a father. I'm determined to fall in love, real love, over the next few months."

"But Del is–"

"Don't go there. I told you what his brother said." Nola stepped back and looked across the room. Del remained where she'd left him, sitting and talking to Dr. Oliver Goodman, her OB doctor! "Oh no!" She couldn't move her feet, but she managed to wildly point.

Holly grabbed at her as if she'd gone into labor. "What's wrong?"

Nola glared straight ahead. Thank God Holly saw what Nola pointed at. "Yikes! I'll drag Olie onto the dance floor."

Holly dashed across the room like some mad woman, ignoring the strange looks from all the guests, and all Nola could do was watch and nod. She, Rusty, Holly and a select few in the OB clinic were the only ones who knew about her pregnancy from the beginning. At the time, it didn't seem to matter who learned of her situation. However, she had no idea the baby's father would cross the world to descend on her life like a royal net.

But now she wondered how on earth she was going to keep her baby a secret–and keep the net from trapping her.

Del leaned back and watched Holly whisk Dr. Goodman away from the table. She seemed a bit odd at times, but he surmised she was a nice woman if she was a friend of Nola's. He'd merely been speaking to the doctor about the new microscope his firm was working on, and before he knew it, the man was gone in a blur of gray pinstriped suit and Holly's pink gown.

He looked up to see Nola standing across the room looking at him. Earlier he'd enjoyed her watching him, anything to get her interested even if she was annoyed at him, but now she seemed upset. He pushed back his chair and headed toward her.

"*Chéri*? What is wrong?" Del came within inches of Nola before she seemed to comprehend he was there. Actually, she was acting strange today. It must be because of him interrupting her wedding, although he'd do it again in, what was it the Americans said, a heartache? No, beat, a heartbeat.

Nola slowly pulled her gaze from across the room and looked as if she only now realized he'd spoken to her. "What? Did you say something?"

"I asked if you were all right?"

"Fine." She clutched the back of a chair as if she was not fine, but he didn't want to argue.

"No stomach problems?"

Her eyes grew unusually round. He'd swear he noted fear in the azure depths although he had no idea what she should be afraid of. The urge to take her into his protective hold was more than he could control. As he reached for her, she shoved at his hands, and said, "What do you mean? My stomach?"

He held his hands at his sides. "You are confusing me, *chéri*, and if I say so myself, I have a fair command of your language."

She softened and said, "Your accent is...I've never had a problem understanding you. I just wanted to know why you asked about my stomach."

"Because of your earlier episode with nausea."

"Oh."

Suddenly she looked so innocent, he wanted to touch her again, even if only for a second. He decided to change the subject of her stomach since talking about it seemed to upset her. "That song, 'The Days of Wine and Roses,' it is a favorite of mine." She gave him a questioning look as if wondering how he knew the American song. But he didn't allow her time to ask. "Please do me the honor, *chéri*." He reached for her hand, but she pulled away.

"No. I don't think we should–"

Del leaned near her ear and sang in a whisper, "The days of wine and..."

Oh geez, she'd forgotten he could sing. "Maybe just one time around the hall."

He smiled to himself in the softness of her voice as he led her toward the dance floor. "Your guests seem to be enjoying themselves," he said, snaking his arm around her shoulder, and hoping she would barely notice–and not shove it off. She didn't. But beneath the soft skin, skin he'd dreamt of running his fingers across these past few months, tense muscles told him she wanted to pull free of his hold. She remained. He smiled, again.

Nola looked at the blur of her friends and Rusty's family dancing around them. It was hard to decipher who was who since right now all she could think about was Del's arms. They felt so wonderful, strong and protective around her. "Yes, they are enjoying themselves," she managed with a great deal of effort.

Her thoughts drifted elsewhere, to his hands moving down her back. He didn't hold too tight, but with the right amount of pressure made his presence known. She felt lightheaded. A giddiness filled her thoughts as if she'd drunk too much of the wine in the song. The band continued to play and unfortunately, she sighed, Del knew all the words.

Maybe it really was a favorite of his. It didn't surprise her that he had a very good singing voice, either. She sneaked a peek at his face. No, nothing about the prince surprised her any longer. A heady feeling had her sink into his hold when she wanted to–knew she should–pull away.

But old memories, special memories, couldn't be ignored.

The wine flowed in the song as intoxicating sensations bombarded her inside. Within hours, her orderly world, the secure world of Soledad, had been torn into tiny bits. How could one man have the power to change her life so? Frightening, she thought, it was truly frightening as Del's hot breaths seared into her skin, and, God help her it was wonderful.

In an attempt to distance her thoughts from him, she inhaled to clear her mind. But, instead of clarity, she got a mega dose of his cologne. It'd been *his* scent from the minute she'd met him at the inservice he had presented for the American delegation of OR staff in Mirabella.

Later she'd learned the fragrance had been specifically created for His Royal Highness by a perfumery in France. No one else in the world could wear the spicy, yet sweet in a masculine sort of way, scent. Something so specific was hard to ignore, and made it near impossible to distance herself from the enticement of the aroma–as impossible as it was to ignore the jolt of her heart each time she inhaled.

"A nickel for your thoughts, *chéri*," he whispered too near her ear for her liking.

She couldn't help a soft laugh that sneaked out. "Penny."

"Hm?"

"It's a penny for your thoughts, and I...my mind was resting." *Resting*? Her brain was in a tailspin with all the damn signals bombarding it from Del's touch, words, heck, even the slight pressure on her back that he insisted on increasing as if she wouldn't notice. She tried to look away, but with every attempt to turn, he'd move and the possible feat would become impossible.

She gave up and looked directly at him. Luckily he'd chosen that moment to look at the band, leaving her to stare at his profile, his sculpted profile, the bones of his jaw, firm beneath the smoothly shaven tawny skin. His hair, darker than any black she'd ever seen, reminded her of the time she, Rusty, and Holly had gone down into a cavern here in New Mexico and the tour guide momentarily turned off the lights to show what total darkness was like.

Del's hair was threads of silken total darkness.

He swirled her around, and this time her stomach didn't lurch about as it had before she ate. Thank goodness the dizziness and nausea usually kept under control after a full meal. She looked up and repeated, "It is a penny for your thoughts."

"Ah, that is correct. My error, most likely caused by inflation."

Nola laughed and caught his fragrance once again. "You've never changed your cologne." She hadn't meant for that to come out. It should have remained a foolish thought.

He pulled her closer. "I know how much you liked it." She wiggled loose. "Do you remember how you wanted to know where I bought it when we first me?" He reached for her hand and swung her closer.

"Yes," she said on a sigh.

"You'd left Mirabella too soon, you know. I had planned to take you to France to have your own fragrance created. Of course," he said, leaning near, "you always smell delicious to me."

His damned fragrance floated on the currents, wrapping his scent around her mind, her heart, only to fill her thoughts with a wine much sweeter than the most expensive champagne. Her knees weakened with each breath. She had to pull away, or who knew where this would lead?

Face it, Nol, you know exactly where it would lead as it did four months ago.

Against all logic, she wanted exactly that, yet cursed her traitorous body and eased free. This was not good, she thought. Nope, not good at all. She had to keep things under her control. "You know the conference was over. I had to return to Soledad."

He looked as if he knew she'd used that as an excuse. Knowing his contacts, he probably had snooped enough to find out that she'd come back a week early. No doubt Henri could pry that information out of a locked vault.

"You left so abruptly."

I had to get away...from you, she thought. "Time is money. I needed to get back to work."

He smiled. She guessed he'd forced it to seem nonchalant. "It has been a while, but I thought you had said you were staying another week when we first met."

Oh damn, he's got a mind like the computers Mirabella exports. And he wasn't fooling her with his, "It has been awhile," routine. Del could probably remember the day of his birth. "No. No, I'm sure I had told you correctly. I was leaving on the ninth—"

"But you left on the second, *chéri*."

Nola pulled loose. "What difference does the date make? I left." And thank God I did, she told herself. "I'm getting tired."

He looked concerned as he placed a steady hand against her back. "Shall we sit?"

"No. I really have to go, Del."

"I think you do not, *chéri*, but I won't prevent you, this time."

Nola didn't stop to look back. She hurried to the front entrance, not caring that she didn't have a car. Nothing in the world could keep her here, so near him. So near that she could barely breathe as his royal web wrapped tighter around her. She shoved at the door, ran down the stairs hailed a cab to head back to her apartment, all the while hearing Del's words in her mind. He wasn't going to pack up and leave, and this time, she couldn't run from him.

He'd invaded her town, her home, her mind.

Nola's supervisor, Ann Priner, motioned for Nola to sit as she entered the head nurse's office the following Monday. Ann was on the phone, so Nola took a seat across from the desk and looked out the window.

A flock of pigeons landed on a statue of St. Lucy near the garden. She leaned back and watched them disappear after splitting off in different directions, shooting into the clouds nearly faster than her eyes could see. Old Stanley, one of the hospital's housekeepers, would have a fit that pigeons were on the statue. Right now, though, watching the birds helped her forget her wedding fiasco—her need for a man.

"Nola?"

"Hm?" She sat up. "Sorry, Ann."

"No problem. I would think that after the day you had Saturday, you'd be a little preoccupied. Holly gave me all the gory details. Sorry your wedding didn't work out."

"Thank you."

Ann leaned nearer. "For what it is worth—and I know I shouldn't be giving personal advice—but I like you, Nola. You're and excellent OR nurse, and top-notched woman." She sat back and said, "You wouldn't have been happy."

Nola sighed. "I know."

"Yet you were willing to marry Rusty?"

Sucking in a deep breath, she said, "I only wanted what was best for my child."

"I understand, but maybe no father is better than just anyone."

"No, that can't be true." She looked at her supervisor. "Rusty would have made a good father."

"No doubt. The guy's a doll." Ann stood and walked to her file cabinet. "But would he have made you a good *husband*?"

"No." The word came out before she had time to think. Although it was the truth, she didn't like hearing it out loud. Now she was back to square one and only had five months left to find a father for her child–and this time she didn't intend to leave any room for errors. She'd make certain she loved whomever she picked, refusing to admit that she'd set a pretty tough goal. But when it came to her baby, nothing was too tough to work for.

Right now, though, she had no one in mind, nor any idea how she was going to accomplish this feat.

"Are you certain you want to cancel your vacation and come back to work?"

"Yes, ma'am. I need to keep busy, and I love my work." She didn't want to tell her boss that she also needed to be out in the work force to look for a prospective husband. New surgeons, anesthesiologists, and other healthcare workers were always coming around since, despite the size of Soledad, St. Lucinda's was a regional hospital. Maybe she'd meet someone and fall madly in love over the next few months. She rolled her eyes and caught Ann staring. Quickly, she forced a smile.

"You are one of my best nurses, Nola. So, since you have chosen to cancel your vacation–" She fished into the file cabinet and pulled out a folder. As she dropped it on the desk in front of Nola, she said, "I'm giving you a 'gravy' assignment."

Nola smiled. "Thank you, ma'am, but there's no need. I'll be fine back in the OR." Keeping busy. Keeping my mind off Del.

"I know you will, but I also know you will do a great job with this assignment. You have the past experience. Besides, light work will be best for you."

Nola nodded.

Ann waved her hand toward the folder. "Take it for review. You'll be assigned over the next few weeks to our guest. He's come here to give an inservice and to check on the equipment his company manufactures...."

Nola watched in horror as the Ann's lips moved. She could have shut her eyes, if that wouldn't be construed as insubordination, and still known what was coming next. She yanked her mind back to her boss in time to hear her say, "He is also a prince, so you refer to him as His Royal Highness Delmar Dupre." Gravy? Gravy, indeed. Ann might as well have dropped Nola into an entire pot of bubbling gray.

"Del."

"Nola, I wouldn't be so informal with visiting royalty, unless he instructs you to call him as such."

Nola sank into her seat. "Yes, ma'am." *No doubt my baby's father won't insist I refer to him as anything else. Heck, I've called him a lot less informal names back in Mirabella.* "Is there anything else?" *Not that there could be after you've already ruined my life.* Obviously Holly had missed telling Ann the main gory detail of which it was that had wrecked Nola's wedding.

"His Highness is staying in the Hillside Arms. Convenient to your place. It would be nice of you to show him around the town, too." Ann, who'd been like a mother to Nola for the past four months, leaned near. Nola thought her boss winked as she said, "I hear he's quite a *looker*."

"You don't say." Standing, Nola made it to the door, nodded, opened it and walked out.

Once outside Ann's office, Nola collapsed against the wall. Could things get any worse?

"Are you all right, *chéri*?"

What were the odds that one of the doctors had taken to calling her by the French term? She opened one eye to see "The Looker" inches from her face. *Things just got worse.* "I will be when you give me some room to breathe." She pushed against his chest, regretting her action as her fingertips touched firm muscles. *Man, these reactions had to stop. It'd been years since she'd studied OB, but maybe the hormones of pregnancy had her libido out of whack. Touching a man should not cause one's fingertips to–sizzle.*

"You're looking pale again. It's not good for you to skip meals, you know."

She curled her lip and said, "Now you're a nutritionist?" when she wanted to inform the nosy prince that she was eating for two.

Wait! She really didn't want to inform him of that!

He chuckled. She let him think she was joking.

It was a matter of survival, because she could never risk telling the truth to someone so wealthy, so powerful, and devious enough to find her at the exact moment to stop her wedding–someone with the means and the power to take away her baby.

Chapter Four

"No, I am not a nutritionist, *chéri*, but it doesn't take a trained eye to see you look a bit pale. I associated it with missing a meal," Del said as Nola contemplated what his reaction would be if he found out the real reason that she looked pale these last few months.

Wary of him actually reading her mind, she pulled her thoughts to the matter at hand.

"I actually ate quite a healthy breakfast," Nola said as she slipped out from his hold. He remained staring at her, as if he didn't believe her. She guessed that's what he thought by the way that he smiled at her. *Whoa.* Even a forced smile did a number on her. Thank goodness the wall was inches behind, she thought, leaning against it for support.

"Good. But it is near noon, and I would like to invite you to lunch."

She wanted to say no. She wanted to get away from his nearness. She wanted to have him gone, so looking at the folder in her hands, feeling a wave of nausea, she said, "I don't think that's a good idea." She hurriedly said, "By the way, I'm assigned to be your–" It was hard to get the word out. She sucked in enough air to finish and said, "–assistant while you're here."

Damn the cocky look in his eyes. "Henri would be proud."

She laughed despite how she hated, and a bit feared, having to spend time with Del. "I won't attempt to fill his shoes. Come on, I'll show you around the OR suite."

"Wonderful." That stupid twinkle sparkled from his eyes.

He loved this. For a fleeting second she wondered if Ann Priner had been bought off. Was that a Rolex she'd been wearing? Forcing the ridiculous thought from her mind and chalking being assigned to Del up as one more streak of bad luck in the life of Nola St. Clair, she said, "Don't get too excited. I'm only assigned during work hours. I have no intention of spending anymore time with you then that–especially after hours. Get that straight, *Your Highness.*"

"But I believe Ms. Priner had mentioned that someone would show me around the town. She said how lovely and quaint Soledad is. A great get away."

He was one slick prince. "If there was a tour bus, I'd give you their phone number. Since there isn't and Ann suggested...I'll give you the nickel tour–"

"Nickel tour?"

"It means I'll show you around. The nickel part means it'll be a short tour." The good prince stood with his huge dark eyes staring at her. She thought of giant chocolate truffles. Creamy. Rich. Delicious. Sometimes she just wanted to hug him as if he was an adorable child, but she remembered her own child growing inside and resisted. Thank goodness she learned not to be impulsive as a kid. Thinking things through saved her hours of punishment and now would save her sanity. His eyes melted into her. "Make that a real short tour."

"Please allow me to treat you to lunch."

"No."

"Don't make this so hard. I feel bad about–"

"Then you shouldn't have objected at my wedding."

He gave an annoying sigh. "We've been through this, and as I said, I'd do it again. Someday you'll thank me."

"Don't bet on it."

"Let me buy you lunch, Nola. What's the harm in that?"

"Okay. Okay. Just this once." Why hadn't she packed a yogurt today? She'd take him to Poncho Salvatore's and order anything with the word *grande* in it. Oh big deal. Ordering the most expensive meal would probably make him feel good. She kept forgetting that money was no object to the prince.

Especially when he wanted his own way.

He took her arm as they walked up the stairs. Her instinct to pull away was overruled by the thought that he'd be near in case she happened to slip. Halfway up, she regretted her logic. His hand on her arm was an annoyance she tried to ignore. But how do you ignore a sizzling touch? Good thing she had his support though. The steps looked slippery. Man, she was doing a good snow job on herself. This rationalizing had to stop. Who knew what would happen if she let it go on until he left?

A better question was, how long would that be?

Hopefully before she started to show.

"We'll go to a local Mexican restaurant. Good food. Reasonable prices."

"That sounds fine, but let me take you somewhere special."

"As in expensive?"

"If that is the case—"

"Del, I've seen your Porsche, the Mercedes in Mirabella, the palace you call home and, of course, Henri makes no bones about your country being a leading exporter of technology. But just because you can afford something else, doesn't mean we should snub our noses at the best food in town."

"I am not, *chéri*. It is just that Dr. Goodman had mentioned a Phillips's restaurant with French cuisine—"

"Too much butter."

Del looked at her. She wasn't being truthful, but he didn't want to argue. He didn't remember her as being so confusing. Nevertheless, he wouldn't quibble about restaurants. He'd save his ammunition for more important things.

Like getting her to come back to Mirabella.

"Whatever you like, *chéri*. Mexican sounds great."

She turned and walked toward the door. Her white skirt hugged slender hips in all the right places. Actually, Nola's hips seemed a bit fuller than he remembered, but no less interesting. Her legs were firm, reminding him of how she could dive so gracefully like an Olympic athlete from the high-board into the pool at his home. A vision of Nola in the tiny, yet, glamorous black bikini she'd worn had him grasp at a nearby doorknob.

Suddenly his hold gave way. A nurse came through the door as he steadied himself on the doorframe.

"Oh, sir, are you all right?" she asked.

"Fine, *Mademoiselle*, fine." At least I will when Nola comes home with me.

The nurse blinked a few times. He thought she purred, but he turned his glance to Nola in time to catch her growl. She spun around and up the stairs. Her skirt took the breeze in its wake, sending the fabric higher on her legs, but only for a moment.

Yes, he would need all the ammunition he could gather to get the woman to change her mind—that is to allow herself to acknowledge feelings that he knew were deep inside her.He knew it from the moment they had made love months ago.

And after years of training to be the possible leader of his country, Del felt confident in his assessment. Confident and eager to prove himself correct where Magnolia St. Clair was concerned.

However, he admitted, he might have better luck getting a truce from his country's sworn enemies.

Nola wiped her finger across her lip to catch the last of the lettuce from her burrito. It was embarrassing the amount she ate lately, but it beat the first three months of nausea she'd suffered through. Now, as long as she kept her stomach filled, she was able to enjoy being pregnant. She looked across the table. Del took a sip of his Margarita.

A sudden urge to share her wonderful news with him flitted through her thoughts only to be stopped short by logic. There was no way she could ever tell him, or want to. Damien had made it clear that royalty must marry royalty. With an annoying leer, he'd also mentioned something about there not being any grandchildren born yet. Well that was no concern of hers. The Mirabellans would have to find themselves another heir. A wave of jealousy at the thought of Del and some princess, he'd eventually have to choose, had Nola shove a mouthful of nachos in all at once.

He could arrange himself a world-shattering royal wedding for all she cared. Surely Henri could ferret out the most eligible princess in the neighboring countries. Del wasted his time coming here. With Henri and Del's resources, there should be no stopping him.

The sobering thought had her mind on children instead of brides. Her child. Their child.

How much power did Del have anyway?

She dipped a nacho into the salsa and bit into it. Could he sidestep American law or, worse yet, have the means to hire some fancy lawyer to twist the law in Del's favor? They so often seemed to do that. Could he take her child or at the very least gain joint custody?

He leaned near, wiped a tiny drip of Margarita from his bottom lip with his napkin. Nola grabbed her napkin and twisted it into a pretzel of a knot to keep from helping him out. When he took a forkful of salad, she had to look away. Too much focusing on his mouth.

With a deep sigh, she told herself he was an honest man, a man of principles, a man of wealth but not fixated on power. He would never hurt her or their child. Then she thought of how he showed up at the precise moment to stop her wedding. Against her wishes, she looked at him as she scraped lettuce from her dish and took another forkful.

A clever man used to getting his own way.

He gave her a strange look. One eyebrow rose. He focused on her plate. She looked down to see one morsel of lettuce remained.

"May I order something else for you?"

Her face grew warmer than the chili peppers burning her mouth. "I'm fine."

"Funny how time plays tricks with our memories. I seem to recall you ate like a nightingale in my homeland." He stabbed at his taco salad.

She choked on the minute piece of lettuce. "Your mind is playing tricks on you. I never ate like a bird." Man, he has a mind tighter than a locked vault, and is as observant as an eager student.

"I'm quite certain you survived on salads and–" He looked down at her plate but even Sherlock Holmes couldn't detect what she'd eaten from the spotless crockery. "–I remember Henri remarking that our guest was a vegetarian. Cook had been quite miffed that you didn't enjoy his veal dishes. They are rather remarkable as is his lamb."

Her stomach churned at the thought of veal. She'd forced herself to eat beef and chicken for the baby, but she drew the line at baby calves and woolly lamb. "Was the cook upset? I had no idea. Be sure to apologize for me–" Damn. She'd forgotten to stick to the lie about being a vegetarian.

He grinned, took her hand, silencing her words. "Why the change, *cheri*?"

Swallowing deeply, it took all her concentration to ignore his hand on hers, tightening actually, although by no means painful. She forced a chuckle. "Guess I'm just a bit wishy-washy lately."

He eased her hand toward his cheek, rubbing gently against his smoothly shaven skin. *Man. Man.* Oh, man she'd forgotten her thought.

"What is this wishy-wash?"

"Washy," she murmured. "It means...it means–" He placed a kiss on her palm. I have no idea what it means, she almost said, but caught herself in time to say, "Someone who is wishy-washy can't make up their minds, keeps changing their thoughts...."

"You are not, this how you call, 'wishy-washy' person, Nola. I have never met a more levelheaded woman who knew her own–" He kissed her hand again, only this time, he let his lips linger. When he looked up, he finished saying, "–mind. You've always struck me as an independent, intelligent woman. How can you say you are this 'washy' person?"

"It's just that–" What the heck is it just?

He turned her hand in his and chuckled. "Tiny cacti."

She looked at her nails. To do one cactus on each nail took longer than the roses. He would notice.

He kissed again–that she noticed.

Oh great. How could she say anything when all she could concentrate on was the third degree burns his hot breath caused on her skin? And she thought the salsa was hot! His touch felt wonderful, but if he put any tongue into it, she'd loose it. He kissed her hand again. She'd never felt anything so magnificent in her life– "Oh!"

Del's eyes widened. "What is it?"

Not able to speak, she waved her hand to signal she was fine. After all, how could she tell him the other most magnificent, wonderful thing had just happened? As she'd been concentrating on Del's touch, the feeling of enjoyment stirred so deep–she felt her baby's first kick.

"Nola, you are frightening me. What is wrong?"

"Nothing. Nothing is wrong." She cursed to herself at how her voice came out so weakly. She swallowed back the words, "The reality of our child just gave me a jolt." Pulling her hand back, she tucked it under the table and rubbed gently across her abdomen to assure her baby that she felt its presence. "I really am fine. A minor twinge is all. Perhaps I did eat more than I'm used to. I'm tired, too. Can't wait 'til the end of the day to go home and rest–"

"I see." But she knew he didn't, or maybe, by the way his glare nearly looked through her, he saw more than she was wanted him to. She turned away, saddened that she couldn't place his hand on her abdomen to feel their child's kick.

Nola shoved her napkin on the table. She had to get out of here. "All set?"

He looked at his Margarita. "I still have half–"

Before he could take another sip, she pushed away from the table, grabbed her purse and turned. "Take your time." Over her shoulder she said, "I'll meet you by the car."

She hurried out, away from his lips, away from the man who had nearly confused her enough to say what she never intended, away from having to keep her secret from him.

Del stood as Nola hurried out of the room. In her rush, she probably didn't noticed him get up. Since she'd turned toward the ladies' room instead of the front door, he seated himself back down, taking a sip of his drink.

Nola had been acting strange since the day he interrupted her wedding. He had no doubt.

He watched the other patrons enjoying their lunch and wondered if his memory of her had been just that. More memory than fact. Perhaps she really wasn't acting any differently? Maybe his mind was playing tricks on him?

Leaning forward, he inhaled a whiff of her cologne that lingered on her napkin. Gently, as if it were made of glass, he lifted it and held it to his face. With a deep sigh, he told himself that there really was never a question in his mind. He knew he'd come here to get the woman who had taken his heart back to the States with her.

There was no mistaking his feelings or his memories.

However, she was acting differently and he intended to find out why. Resisting the urge to pocket the napkin, he placed it onto the table, stood and walked toward the door.

Beep. Beep.

Before he made it outside, he looked down at his watch. Henri materialized.

"Your Highness."

51

"No need to bow on this thing," Del said, knowing Henri was doing that although he couldn't see all of his portly body. Suddenly his pulse began to speed beneath his watch. He'd already checked in with Henri once today and feared news of his father. News that would not be good. "Is my father–"

Henri waved, despite the tiny screen only allowing him to be seen from the shoulders up. "No. No, Your Highness. Nothing is wrong with Prince Leon. That is, all is the same."

The sense of relief that had started with Henri's words, turned to worry. "Good. Then what is it, Henri?"

"I hope that I am not interrupting something important, but the queen asked me to check on you."

Del felt his eyebrows raise amid a deep sigh. "I am fine, although I know she doesn't mean for you to be checking on my health." Henri grew ruddy, and this time Del knew nothing was wrong with the TV's color. "She is inquiring how soon I will be back in Mirabella?"

"*Oui.*"

"I knew she couldn't keep out of this. She'd made it clear about Nola. Her Royal Highness needs to get a few things straight."

Henri seemed to choke on his words. "Please, Your Highness, I cannot–"

Del chuckled. "I do not intend for you to wage my battles with my father's wife. I will handle her interference."

"Thank you."

Del chuckled. "My plans to marry differ from Queen Francine's plans. But no matter. With the good luck that the clerics of the court had been bestowed upon me at my birth, I shall succeed–soon."

Del thought he noticed a twinkle in Henri's eyes despite the tiny screen. "*Mademoiselle* St. Clair. She has agreed–"

"Easy does it, Henri. She merely agreed to share a meal with me. She's...not very cooperative. It seems I may be here a bit longer than expected. Having her face reality is going to be tougher than I had anticipated. Actually, you might rearrange my schedule so I can stay here longer. Say, a week or two. Will that be a problem?"

Henri paused then said, "No, sir. I...can arrange it."

"You hesitate, Henri. Is it because of the cartel?"

"*Oui.*"

Del sighed. "I know they are like wolves at our door, but I need more time. Keep them away from my father lest they notice him acting–differently. Our country needs that deal to go through."

"More than ever. The recent rains have flooded many vineyards. Farmers are loosing their crops and soon after they'll lose the land of their birth. With the cartel agreement, Mirabella's export prices will be maintained and our production can increase, giving jobs to thousands who cannot work in the factories."

But not if the cartel looses faith in our ruler, Del thought. Henri must find it too difficult to say that the king he had served under so loyally and for so many years, could ruin the entire deal if the members of the cartel knew of his condition.

"And, Henri, I don't have to tell you to keep Damien out of it all."

"*Oui.*"

"I will handle things, Henri. Anything else?"

"No, Your Highness. *Au revoir.*"

"*Au revoir*, and, Henri, my father would be very proud of you."

The screen began to dim as Del heard a faint, "*Merci*," from his trusted friend.

"Was that my buddy Henri?"

Del swung around to see Nola standing behind him. "*Oui*...I mean, yes." He shoved his hand to his side as if she could still see Henri. "Have you been here long?"

"Nope." She gave him a questioning look. "It's not as if I was eavesdropping, you know."

Del rarely felt flustered. He left that up to Henri, but wondering if Nola had heard his conversation had him off balance. "What is this, dropping Eve?"

She laughed. "Eavesdropping means someone purposefully listening to someone else without their knowledge."

He grew silent, worrying if in fact she had heard and was trying to tell him it wasn't on purpose.

She tucked her arm beneath his and tugged him toward the door. "I didn't hear anything except a faint '*merci*' from Henri." She nudged him in the side, releasing some of his concern by saying,

"Whatever he was thanking you for, I have no idea."

Del managed a chuckle and told himself he was being ridiculous. Henri's reminder of the cartel and his father's condition had him out of sorts.

And a prince must always be able to remain in control with a clear head–unlike poor papa.

Nola tried to ignore Del's preoccupation. She wasn't certain if came from him scrutinizing her during lunch as if she were a store mannequin, or from his phone call to Henri. If she had to make an educated guess though, she'd vote for the later. Something Del's right-hand man had told him seemed to have Del acting oddly.

"Nola?"

She looked upward. Del stood near his car, holding the passenger door open. Normally, she'd mention that she were quite capable of opening the door for herself, but right now her mind was more tossed than the salad Del had eaten with his lunch.

"Thanks." She got in. The leather wrapped its buttery softness around her. The feeling made her quiet sleepy. A nap sounded like a wonderful dessert, but sleeping during the day had always seemed like such a waste. Of course, being pregnant had changed a few things in her life, and feeling tired during the middle of the day was one of them. A yawn sneaked out before she could swallow it back.

"Tired?" Del asked as he pulled out into the street.

"I guess I didn't sleep too well last night." She couldn't tell him that was partly true, since she'd been reliving him stopping her wedding over and over. It seemed like ages ago, and as dear Holly had put, "a fairytale thing to do," or some such nonsense. What a hopeless romantic. "Take a left here, and we'll start your tour."

Del reached into his pocket and fished out something. Without taking his eyes off the road, he handed her a shiny quarter.

"What's this for?"

"My tour."

Nola looked at the coin. "It's supposed to be a nickel."

He pulled to a stop sign and turned to her. The darkness of his eyes deepened to the shade of midnight on a moon-less night. In what had to be the sexiest voice she'd ever heard, including at *R* rated movies, he whispered, "I'll pay five times as much to spend five times as long with you, *chéri*."

Oh man. Why did this guy have to be a prince?

Couldn't her luck ever involve someone as wonderful, as heavenly, as all out sensual as Delmar Dupre to stumble into her life as a plain ordinary man? A doctor would be perfect. Then she could afford to quit her job and stay home with her child. She sighed. "I do have to get back to work, you know." Back there was her only chance of finding a father for her baby. Out of the corner of her eye, she looked at Del. The baby kicked again. "We'll settle for a dime's worth."

Del's laugher filled the lush interior of the car, making Nola feel weaker than the fog of sleep that had enveloped her after her big meal. "You've got it. A dime it is."

"We'll start out at the far end of the town. One of my favorite spots."

"Why is that, *chéri*?"

She pointed to turn to the right. "It's the best spot to see the canyons. I love to go on hikes there." But not in my condition for now.

Del reached over and touched her arm. "Then we shall share your spot together."

With a handful of words and one swift movement of the steering wheel, he turned the car and her heart.

Chapter Five

Del watched Nola cautiously walk across the flat rock formation. He'd have expected her to be climbing the folds of stone instead of staying on the fenced path. Perhaps she had eaten too much for lunch? An eagle flew overhead, disappearing into the cottony clouds, leaving the azure sky in silence. "I can see why you enjoy coming here," he said.

Nola nodded and leaned near. "It's peaceful."

He stepped forward. With a weary look on her face, she stepped back. "Out to the left...."

Del watched her give a guided tour of the canyon area, but didn't hear a word she'd said. Instead, he satisfied himself studying her. It'd only been four months since she had walked away from him down the Jetway at the Mirabellan airport, but she really had changed. There was something different in her eyes. Maturity? Hope? He wasn't sure, but it was there.

And he wanted to know why.

"So? Any questions?" she asked.

"Hm?" He couldn't tell her that he'd studied her more than the scenery so he smiled and said, "Can't think of any right now." Except maybe what are you hiding?

"Then let's get back."

He reached to take her hand. She pulled away. Holding onto the railing, she walked a bit ahead of him.

Okay, he thought, I'll enjoy this view for awhile.

The wind snatched strands of golden hair from the barrette she wore. When not at work, Nola wore her hair loose. He loved the way it curled under at her shoulders. Her hips really were a bit wider than he remembered–maybe since she ate meat and quite a bit of it lately–but nonetheless, her hips were enticing as they swayed. And by the way his body reacted, they still had the ability to excite him. Quickening his pace before he lost his control, he came shoulder to shoulder with her. She stopped to watch a chipmunk scurry across the path.

"They are so adorable," she said, chuckling.

"Like someone I know."

She shook her head and groaned. A few strands of hair landed near her lips. He watched for a moment. She lifted her hand toward her face most likely to remove the hair, but instead, she paused as he moved closer. "Don't you dare–"

With a gentle touch, he eased the hair free only to have the wind steal it from his hold. "Relax. I'm only keeping you looking more adorable than our little furry friend."

She curled her lip and said, "What a line."

He smiled. "True. Seeing you has my integrity slipping. Besides, I'm saving my big guns for later."

"Don't waste your ammo, Your Highness."

She'd taken to calling him that and not in the most respectful way. Still, he laughed. Respect he got from the Mirabellans. He wanted something entirely different from her. She looked at him and joined him with a laugh. He couldn't help but remember how that sound made him feel. Made him remember. "Your laugh, *chéri*, how I loved to hear it–"

She froze on the path and looked at him. "Don't go there," she said softly.

"I *am* there." He waved his hands outward to encompass the nearby landscape. "It is months ago, *chéri*. We are at our picnic in the Forrest of Maidens by the palace–weeks after meeting." He stepped forward. "We are sharing a picnic of wine, cheese, and the cook's finest vegetable medley." That's right, he thought, she didn't eat meat when he'd first met her. Too enamored of the moment to bring it up, he would let that go for now.

Gently, cautiously, he took her arm. She stiffened under his hold but let herself be turned enough to look at the canyons. "The cliffs overlook the Mediterranean. Picture the vibrant colors. The never-ending waves." She followed his pointing. "Between the giant trees the surf slams into the rocky prominence below. I lay out the blanket–"

"I...remember."

"The memory of that day is so clear in my mind, *chéri*, I have no choice but to relive the scene, the wonderful moment." With that, he leaned down and kissed her on the neck. She stilled. He moved his lips across the delicate skin of the nape of her neck. Wrapping his hold tightly, he turned her around.

58

This time, she pulled back. Before he could apologize, her body relaxed against his chest. Taking her signal as a green light, he leaned down and allowed his lips to taste of Nola once again. She tasted of sweetness from the milk she'd drunk at lunch. When her lips parted to allow his tongue free reign, he tasted the pungent flavor of salsa, the hot, burning spice giving thought to his most animal urges. Her eager tongue touched his, sending his body into a whirlwind of desire. When he ran his hands across her cheeks to tuck the errant strands of hair behind her ear, she returned his kiss, this time tasting of the past, of magnificent memories, of the uniqueness of his Nola.

He could care less what Queen Francine thought.

Nola's hands slid between them, giving a gentle shove. "We have to stop," Nola said in a somewhat hoarse voice. He chalked it up to the affects of their kiss—and smiled. "I need to get back to work."

"I don't want to get you into any trouble."

Nola sighed. Too late, she thought, rubbing her abdomen. Ambivalent feelings caused a sadness in her heart. She'd be ecstatic to share the news with Del if she knew they could plan a life together. That dream's impossible, she thought sadly. With a gentle shove to his shoulder, she eased past, heading to the car. She opened the door for herself and sank into the leather seat. "We'll head toward the east. You can see the western ridge. The upper peak looks like George Washington's profile. It's really neat," she rambled on through the open window.

He stood a few minutes as if unsure how to move. She had to pull her gaze from him. He looked too damn good with the wind tossing his hair about. His eyes held a glassy stare. A slight redness formed on his lips.

God how she wanted to jump out of the car and run to him.

Thank goodness he finally moved and got in. Once in his seat, he turned. "I will not apologize for something that I enjoyed so much—and that I think you did as well."

Nola didn't want to tell him how she agreed with his comment. Over the past few months she'd managed to convince herself that her feelings for Del were a mere infatuation. A product of a whirlwind courtship fueled by the romance of a foreign country, the intrigue of meeting someone of wealth, and, she couldn't deny, the absolute seduction of the most handsome, kind, loving man she'd ever met.

But today her convictions wavered.

"Take a left near that giant cactus," she managed before they took a wrong turn. She sure as heck didn't want to get lost our here with him.

Del eased the car along the road with the slightest of efforts. Perhaps fancy expensive cars practically drove themselves.

"Let me see. I have about six and half cents left on my tour. Where to next?"

"I really want to get back to the hospital—"

"You would cheat me so?"

She shook her head and clicked her tongue. On a deep sigh, she said, "Okay. Okay. I'm not a cheapskate. I have to go to the grocery store. It's very quaint in a western sort of motif. That'll have to qualify for part of your tour."

"Sounds fine. I'm fascinated by things new to me."

"It's not that very different from most stores. A few cacti, red chili pepper wreaths and cattle skulls decorate the outside. No big deal."

"It will be for me, since I've never been to any kind of grocery store...."

She knew he was speaking, but her mind couldn't fathom the thought of someone never going shopping for food. Not that she didn't believe Del. She knew with the number of servants at the palace he wouldn't have any reason to run to the local store for a gallon of milk. The stark reality of Del's revelation only added fuel to her conviction that they could never belong together.

A man who had never shopped—a woman who at one time could barely afford food—they definitely came from two different worlds.

Once at the store, Nola grabbed a cart near the door. "I only have a few things to get but this is a grocery cart. You stick your purchases in it."

Del gave the shopping cart a once over and chuckled. "I look forward to shopping with you, *chéri*."

"Don't get used to it. This is a one-time treat to make you a well-rounded person."

Del looked at his waistline. "I surely do not want to be as well-rounded as Henri."

Nola laughed. "This is going to be some trip."

He stepped forward. She hesitated. "What now?"

He covered her hand with his. "May I?"

After several blinks she realized what he wanted. "Knock yourself out," she said as she let him take control of the cart. "Don't run into anything or anyone."

He laughed and wheeled the cart down the produce aisle. Amid Del's amazement of how neatly oranges could be stacked in the display counters, how one slab of meat could be sliced like paper, and how several aisles were specifically designated to "junk food" as she had pointed out, Nola began to enjoy their trip. She managed to put her worries about finding her baby a father out of her mind long enough for her and Del to chose apples, peaches, and pears without bruises. "You're like a kid in a candy store," she teased.

"This is good? No?"

"It is to the kid." She laughed. "It means you are enjoying yourself as a child who was given free reign in a store full of sweets would be."

Her analogy backfired as he leaned near and whispered, "Nothing could satisfy my sweet tooth like a kiss of your candy red lips."

Oh, man. His hot breath tickled her cheek. She nearly bumped into a pyramid of canned soup. Suddenly this shopping trip had become dangerous. There was something too personal about picking out fruit with a man. Having to watch his large hands run over the smooth skin, pressing, touching, and wishing it was her skin and not some peach's. Dangerous wasn't the word for the desire building inside her. Despite her *grande* meal, she suddenly felt famished. Instead of craving the sweet nectar of a peach, though, she craved the candied taste of Del.

Beep. Beep. Beep.

Nola looked down at Del's watch. "Is something wrong with your watch? It sounds different."

"It's not the watch," he said, lifting a beeper from the inside of his jacket pocket. Before she could ask why he carried a beeper, too, he set it back and pulled another one out of his pants pocket. She watched as he read the number to himself and wondered why on earth someone with a TV on their watch would use a beeper too. That is, two beepers. He caught her looking. "Sometimes I forget my watch. Excuse me, *chéri*."

"Sure." He'd always worn his watch, she thought as he walked to the front of the store where he pushed some numbers into it. And two beepers. Maybe matters of one's country were so pressing he needed a backup. She could only guess that he was calling Henri as she pretended to squeeze a few cantaloupes. Having no idea what one was supposed to feel like, she shoved two into her basket and looked up. Del stood near the front door, talking. Henri must be on the other end, but she couldn't tell from here.

She should have paid more attention to lip-reading while doing her nurse's training back in college. Not that she wanted to be nosy about his business, but a feeling of concern, something she couldn't shake despite telling herself she didn't care about him, kept her interested.

From his conversation with Henri the first day she saw his TV watch, she got the niggling suspicion that all was not right in the palace of Mirabella. Oh well, she had to force herself to stay out of Del's life–much like she wanted him to do with hers. She busied herself down the aisle, knowing she was shoving things into her cart that she would never eat. No problem. She'd invite Rusty and Holly over. They'd eat anything.

She looked up to see Del pass by the aisle. "Del, over here," she called as he walked near the coffee.

"I must take care of something." He handed her his car keys and before she could argue, he said over his shoulder, "I'll walk the few blocks to the apartment. You need the car for your purchases. Thanks for the nickel tour."

She looked at the key chain in her hand and murmured, "Dime."

Nola shoved the key into the door of Del's Porsche only to be startled by the screech of an alarm. "Oh great! I should have known." She looked at the darn keys in her hand. Maybe if she ignored it, it would stop. She slung her groceries into the car then jumped in and stuck the key into the ignition. The screech continued, and now several shoppers were staring. Nola jumped out and ran to the pay phone. If Del wasn't back in his room by now, soon the police would be arriving to accuse her of grand theft auto. She shoved in a quarter and dialed.

Thank goodness he answered.

"What's the trick to turning off this car alarm?"

"Oh, *chéri*, I'm sorry."

"Don't waste words, give me the numbers." Del fired off the combination while Nola wrote them on her palm. "Bye!" Before she could hear Del's voice, she slammed down the receiver and ran. After pushing in the numbers, the alarm gave a final beep and silenced. "Oh, man." Nola collapsed into the driver's seat and inhaled the familiar scent of leather.

For a few seconds she merely sat there and thought of how different she and Del really were. By the looks of the custom interior, his car probably cost more than she earned in ten years. She shut her eyes and heard the screeching alarm in her mind as if it were shouting a reminder of their differences. "Okay," she said, opening her eyes. "You've convinced me. Hopefully he'll be leaving soon, and I won't be tempted to...tell him."

The car drove like a dream. Nola told herself it would only be in her dreams that she could afford a Porsche like this. The thought of tightening her budget fast approached. As a single nurse, she'd enjoyed buying what she needed, when she needed it, unlike the earlier years when she had to make do with very little. Now that a child would become part of her life, though, she had to face buying baby equipment, the cost of disposable diapers since she couldn't fathom using cloth, and saving for a college education. The responsibility all rested on her shoulders. If she found the husband she intended to, at least some of the responsibility would ease.

Ignoring the truth that she might be crazy to set such a goal, she chose to ignore the difficulty of finding a husband–especially one willing to raise another man's child.

Rubbing her abdomen, she enjoyed another kick. "Don't worry, pumpkin, we are going to be fine. Mommy is going to find you a daddy real soon. And, if not, the two of us will manage." The thought was sobering, yet somehow she knew she was telling her child the truth. She'd never lie about something so sacred to her–not after her childhood nights of crying herself to sleep.

Back at her apartment, Nola started to unload her groceries. As she leaned into the trunk to pull out a bag, she felt someone approach. Assuming it was one of her neighbors, she reached for another bag, ignoring whomever was behind her.

"I see you have put the grocery store to good use," Del said.

Nola swung around. A bag of oranges opened, bouncing them out of her hand to roll across the lawn. "You scared me."

"I apologize, *chéri*. I may help?"

"What about your business?"

He hesitated and looked concerned. Something *was* going on. "It is being handled."

"Here." She handed him a bag and stooped to pick up the oranges.

"Let me." Del bent at the same time, rubbing against her shoulder. She told herself to ignore his touch. He bumped into her hand as they reached for the same orange. She told herself the sun caused the heat on her skin. Finally one orange remained. Nola paused.

She knew Del's manners would have him reaching for it, so she did, too. She told herself she was being polite, but when he took her hand into his, bent, and gently kissed along her arm, she told herself she was full of bologna–her darn body wanted him to touch her!

Del picked up the orange and tucked it into her bag. He glared at her for a moment, nearly knocking her back from her kneeling position. She purposefully pulled herself up. "Thanks. I'll go put my groceries away and call you later for a ride back to the hospital to get my car–"

"Allow me to help."

She should say no. She should just turn around and say it over her shoulder. She should not come within ten feet of the Royal Intruder if she wanted to keep her mind from turning to mush. She managed a weak, "I'll be fine."

Of course he didn't fall for that. "You don't want to cheat me out of the grand finale of the tour. I must see how a shopping expedition is completed."

"For crying out loud. You shove the groceries into the cabinet. It's not brain surgery."

How could a grown man, a highly educated one with the responsibly of a country on his shoulders pout like a three year old?

One day she'd be looking at her three-year-old, who might very well look exactly like his father. "Okay," she mumbled.

Once inside her apartment, she knew she'd made a mistake. Del scrutinized each item as she pulled it from the bag. A huge mistake.

"You'd think those were precious jewels instead of fruits and veggies," she teased.

He chuckled. "Jewels do not interest me, *chéri*."

Was that really true? Could someone who grew up a prince *not* be interested in the perks of the position? What does it matter. "Here, stick these in the fruit bin."

He took the apples from her hand. "And the fruit bin would be where?"

"Bottom drawer of the frig." As she turned to pull a can of soup from the bag, she heard him mumble something. "What?"

He stood with the door to the refrigerator open, looking in as if at a museum display. "Why so much milk? I don't remember you drinking–"

She dropped the can back into the bag and pushed at the refrigerator door. "Women need calcium for strong bones. Besides, didn't the queen ever teach you not to look in a woman's refrigerator?"

"I thought that was her purse?"

"The frig is sacred. Besides," she said, shoving the door closed, "you have to close it faster or the cold air comes out and my electric bill skyrockets."

"Sorry. I'll reimburse you for–"

She laughed more to change the subject than because what he said was funny. Actually she had a strange suspicion he was being serious. Del was never stingy, even though she knew he could afford whatever he wanted. She remembered how he'd treated all the staff that had come with her to Mirabella to a weekend on the Mediterranean. Most of them could never have afforded such a luxurious trip. At the time, she wondered if he'd done it to have her all to himself–not that she'd found a thing to complain about–but he had been generous to everyone.

All her fears of leaving Soledad had evaporated in the mist of Del's presence–until Damien had showed up.

It was then she knew that she never should have left home.

"Where does this go?" Del stood there holding a bottle of water.

"Top cabinet on the left."

"Something is wrong with the water in Soledad?"

She chuckled. "No. Occasionally I take bottled water out on my hikes." Oh no. No way did she want him asking why they didn't hike around the canyons today.

Before he had time to ask, she bent to stack the cans of cream of mushroom soup on the bottom shelf. What a Ward and June Cleaver moment this was. Putting groceries away made her think of how nice it would be to have a man to share her life with–only not the man reading the ingredients on her potato chips right now.

Well she'd remedy that soon.

"Okay, give them here. I know they're not the most nutritious things to eat, but a girl needs some vices." With a line like that she should have expected the leer from the prince. Not that she'd intended to say something that could be interpreted two ways, but as he stepped near, she couldn't force an explanation of what she really meant. No, she couldn't manage that when her words keep getting swallowed back down as he came closer, smelling so great. Nor could she think clearly as he lifted her hair from her face, sending tingling sensations down the back of her neck, or when he bent forward, his warm breath steaming the skin on her cheeks.

Oh man, the last thing she wanted right that second was to explain *anything*.

She managed to step back. He filled in the gap real fast.

"You smell wonderful." His lips brushed against hers.

"Hospital aroma–" she muttered dreamily, grabbing onto the counter. "Uniform soaks it up."

He tucked her hair behind her ears, running his large hands against her skin. His touch was gentle, yet with the right amount of pressure to make her reach up and take his hands with hers. She should ease them down to his sides, but he twisted her hold so that his hands were in control, then he kissed the palms of one, then the other. "Your skin is soft as the clouds."

She sighed, knowing that clouds were made of gases, but, damn if his accent didn't make whatever he said sound so...so arousing. "Yeah, clouds–" He took her words with his lips once again. She couldn't care less. Who knew what she was going to say, anyway? It didn't matter. Right now the only thing that mattered was the wonderful feel of his lips on hers, his tongue teasing against her mouth until she opened to invite him inside.

Ward and June never did this on TV. Heck, they slept in twin beds.

What the heck was she doing?

With a swift shove, she separated them and took several steps back–out of inhaling range. You're going to have to do way better than this to get rid of him, she told herself.

"*Chéri–*"

"Don't call me that! And stop kissing me! That is, don't ever kiss me again."

"I won't stop trying to kiss you–when I know you want it as much as–"

She grabbed onto the counter for support again. It was either that or she'd go with her urge to smack him. "Isn't that awfully arrogant of you to assume–"

"A few minutes ago you wouldn't have argued with me on that point. But, okay, I won't try to kiss you."

"Good."

He grinned. "For now."

"Look, Your Highness, we are going back to a strictly professional relationship. No more tours of Soledad, no more little jaunts to the canyons and, I repeat, no more kissing!"

Beep. Beep.

Nola looked at his hand. "Aren't you going to get that?"

"I'd rather continue this conversation, but I must. Excuse me." He bent near his wrist and spoke too softly for her to hear.

"Conversation my eye. Doesn't he even recognize an argument when he's in the middle of one? Talk about leading a sheltered life." She touched at her lips, wondering if she should ever wash off the wonderful feeling. Then she hurried to the sink. With a splash of water to her face, she asked, "Is it Henri?"

"Unfortunately. Too bad beheading is no longer in vogue. I'd rather finish what we'd started earlier."

Ignoring him, she called across the room, "Hey, Henri. How're you?"

The assistant seemed frozen on the screen. "Um. Fine, *Mademoiselle* Nola. I am sorry to interrupt but–"

A female voice pierced the screen. "Nola? Nola? Not that American–"

Del pulled his hand away from Nola. Anger filled the depths of his eyes as he looked at the queen. "Yes. Nola St. Clair is here."

"Hello, Your Royal Highness," Nola said, not close enough to think the queen could hear.

"What are you doing with her, Delmar?" Queen Francine asked.

"Did you want something?"

"Why else would I have this man call you?"

Nola worried the screen might crack with the piercing tone of the queen's voice.

"That man's name is Henri. You know that."

Nola smiled at the protective tone Del used for Henri. She'd sensed a bond between the two the first time she'd seen them together. Surely he could be trusted with the deepest of Del's secrets.

"Whatever. I want to know what is going on with the cartel."

Thank goodness the subject is off her, Nola thought. She'd never been on the queen's list of favorite Americans as far as she could tell. Instead of eavesdropping, she bent to re-stack her soup cans. Luckily Del hadn't mentioned how many cans of cream of mushroom she'd bought like the stupid milk. Since the early days of morning sickness, she'd grown a fondness for that soup. Of course that may have been because it was the only thing she could keep down.

"Is something wrong, Your Royal Highness?" Del asked rather tersely.

Nola peered over a can of soup. Odd that Del didn't call the queen something more familiar, like "mother." Then again, maybe Nola was too sensitive where mothers were concerned.

"Your assistant tells me you want to stay there longer."

Nola's ears perked up. She shouldn't be listening, especially when Del covered the screen with his hand. Although by the sound of things, she wished she couldn't hear.

Oh, man, he was going to be here longer?

"I will discuss this with you tonight. I will call around nine your time–"

"Your father is going to hear about this, Delmar."

"Leave him out of this," he said firmly.

Nola guessed his tone wasn't only annoyance.

"Good day, Your Highness. Henri, will you stay on the line a moment?"

Nola heard a faint "*Oui*" as she continued to stack. The tower of tin was getting too high, but she couldn't pull herself from the job. Then she'd have to leave the room.

If Del planned to be around here longer, she sure wanted to know. It'd take more than sidestepping to get away from him. After the stupid kisses, she had to yank in her foolish desires and keep a clear head. The top of the tower teetered.

As if she weren't in the room, Del walked toward the hallway and around the corner. Hm. He didn't want her to hear.

The tower swayed, toppled. "Ouch!" Nola yelled as she quickly picked up the cans of soup that had landed against her shin. "This is ridiculous," she muttered, hobbling over to the refrigerator for a piece of ice. "It's my damn apartment. He can use his watch in his car if he has so many secrets to keep."

Cold touched her hand. Del's voice came through the doorway, "It shouldn't be too hard to do, Henri, since the two are so into themselves. But, I beg of you, keep Damien *and* Queen Francine away from my father."

Chapter Six

Nola realized her hand was still in the refrigerator. A piece of ice froze itself onto her fingertips. She pulled her hand out, bent, shoved the ice onto her shin and wondered why Del would want to keep the queen away from the king.

As cold water trickled down her leg, it occurred to her that they were rarely together when she was their guest. Several servants had mentioned in passing that they had to attend to the queen in her chambers. Nola remembered laughing at the fact that anyone called his or her room "chambers" in this day and age. That's right though, she thought, the king and queen did use separate parts of the palace.

How odd. But even odder, was Del telling Henri to keep them away from each other. Geez, was there no end to his secretiveness? Damien she could understand–the snake. That prince's personality was obvious even on first meeting. King Leon always seemed a bit off when Damien was around, too.

Well, Nola St. Clair was no fool. Now she really had her work cut out. She'd gotten the impression months ago that Del was the favorite son of his father and Damien of their mother. That made it clearer why Del had so much more control over decisions about his country. Of course, anyone could see Damien was only out for himself.

She'd at least give Del credit for being a good businessman and concerned royal.

A twinge in her lower abdomen took her mind off him for a second. She eased to stand, her pulse starting to race. After a few seconds and a flutter of the baby, she took a deep breath, certain everything was all right. As her pulse slowed to normal, she looked up to see Del staring. Oh, man. What kind of excuse was she going to give him now? She sank back into her chair.

"I will call later, Henri." He shoved his finger at a button on his watch and moved closer. "What is wrong?"

"Hm? Wrong? Nothing. I'm fine." Nola turned her head downward, certain her heated cheeks were as red as the soup can label.

He eased her face up with a finger under her chin and looked at her hand holding the ice against her shin. "If nothing is wrong, why are you icing your leg?"

"The cans fell."

"I see that, but you were as pale as your white cabinets. I'm beginning to worry about your health. Are you certain you are not ill?"

Pregnancy is not an illness, she thought, despite feeling rotten for the first three months. "I'm not sick. Guess the pain had me a bit nauseous. Everything all right back home?"

The diversion worked. Del shook his head in what she read as disgust. With raised eyebrows he said, "Nothing I can't handle."

A twinge of disappointment struck Nola that he didn't tell her what was going on. She argued with herself that it didn't matter. She had no ties to Del. A man in his position obviously couldn't be discussing business with an American—a commoner no less.

"Let me see your shin." He looked downward.

She covered one leg with the other. "It's fine." He stepped near. "Don't get so close, Del. I warned you before—"

Nola swallowed to give herself time to think. But like the trained strategist he was, Del walked closer—determined. He touched his hand to her shoulder. She tried to stand. "I know a lot about bruises, *cher*– Nola. I played a lot of sports in college."

Her attention waned. "Soup can induced bruises are not the same as football–"

His chuckle, like a royal net, wrapped around her, taking her focus. What was it she was going to say?

"You really are as adorable as the little chipmunk. Let me take a look...."

First she felt the strong hand lift her leg. She watched his eyes study her skin that merely had a red mark on it, most likely from the ice. Then, in an obvious calculated move, he brushed his lips against hers as he gently lowered her leg.

Damn!

She pushed a hand to his chest. "You'd never make it as a doctor, Your Highness." No match for his strength, he remained much too close—despite her efforts to distance herself.

"Ah, but I would certainly enjoy my practice." With a leer, he pulled her to his chest. With that, he kissed her.

Nola couldn't argue for the few seconds her heart leapt and her body cried out for more.

The baby chose that moment to practice its punches. Thank goodness. The tiny fist pulled her back to reality. She pulled her head back, pushed on his chest. He let her go. Hopefully Del hadn't felt the baby! Pausing, she watched his reaction. Nothing as far a suspicion. Good. "I made myself clear when I left Mirabella."

Del stared at her for several seconds. Why couldn't she see how they felt about each other? Feel the chemistry. Know they were perfect for each other. He let her move further away. Slowly she eased near the counter, never taking her eyes off of him. He smiled. "You watch me as if in fear that I will grab you again–"

"You don't scare me, Del."

"Hm, then perhaps I misread the look in your eyes, Nola. Maybe it is because you don't trust yourself. Maybe you fear running back into my arms. I choose to believe the later."

"Damn you–"

"Maybe you scare yourself with wanting me."

"You arrogant–"

He laughed. "Some would say that. But I like to call being able to read your looks so accurately–intuitive."

"Stop trying to guess what I'm thinking and hear this. We do not, nor can we ever belong together. I said it months ago, and I'm repeating it now to save you from having to read my mind."

"I will never forget what you said when you left." His eyes grew serious. "Nor will I ever believe the words." He took a step back to give her space. "You see everything in black and white, Nola. Sometimes life hands us gray. Sometimes we have to allow ourselves to see past the fine lines to the areas that blend into one another. For me, everything is not so clear-cut. Like a masterpiece, the colors blend, mingle."

She hesitated, then said, "You're right. I do see black and white and it is plainly clear to me that we can never belong together."

But Del saw doubt in her eyes. He'd never known her to be the nervous type, but right now she taped her finger on the aqua Formica counter, the nails clicking in the silent room. "Don't chip the tiny cacti, *chéri*." She glared at him. Nola wasn't even able to convince herself that she didn't want him–but he wouldn't point that out.

No need to anger her further.

He'd always believed his father's advice that an opponent would reveal their weakness in time–not that he thought Nola weak. No, he'd never met a woman stronger in character and prowess. But what he was banking on right now was waiting until she weakened to the truth–then he could move in to win the battle.

She looked uncomfortable standing there. He had no intention of making her feel that way in her own home so he said, "I believe I have about three cents worth left on my tour."

Her stiff shoulders relaxed. "Neutral territory. Suits me." She glared at him a second. "Let me stick those cans back in the cabinet and we'll head over to the hospital."

Del smiled and bent to help her with the cans. At first she looked as if she'd push him out of the way, but instead, she said a quiet, "Thanks." He shoved the cans inside, wondering about her taste in soup, but decided not to question her in case she got angry again–or made up another lie–like the one about the milk.

He followed her out of the apartment toward the car, stealing a few peeks at her bottom. Yes, much fuller he was convinced, yet still–enticing.

Once at the hospital, Nola introduced Del to Dr. Framer, the head of surgery, who invited him into his office to discuss the new equipment. She then stole a few minutes to herself, collapsing on the couch in the nurse's lounge. Thank goodness no one was here right now.

No way would she want to have to explain why she felt so crummy. She should be thrilled about the baby, and she was, but Del's unexpected visit and all that it entailed had brought her carefully laid out plans to a screeching halt.

It would be so easy to ignore him if he weren't so damned gorgeous, so blasted wonderful, or so doggoned perfect.

Maybe he wasn't even human.

She took a deep breath. Her thoughts kept getting weirder. Well, maybe not. No one was that perfect. She'd seen Del in all his royal glory, but everyday living could be a different matter. Maybe someone that looked so good had to put way too much time into appearance, and would make a selfish father. That made her feel better.

Del might not even like children. Of course he'd need an heir for his country, but no way would she ever allow her child to be born into that situation.

Every child deserved love.

Not position. Not responsibility.

Maybe she was worrying for nothing. If Del found out about the baby, he might not accept it. Knowing him, he might make a token donation to its college fund and hightail it out of her life. Maybe a commoner having his baby would stir too much gossip in Mirabella. She tapped her nail to her tooth, careful not to chip the cactus, and wondered if she should tell him. That might be his incentive to change his mind about leaving.

Then again, growing up a prince he probably got whatever his little heart desired.

Would he desire their child?

He did have a way of wrapping some invisible web around her. That she couldn't deny. And look what kind of effect he had on Holly.

What would he do to take control of their child's life?

Nannies. Boarding school. Leaning back, she shut her eyes. God, this was all so exhausting. It wouldn't take much to fall asleep, but she did have another hour of work to do. Besides, she didn't trust the dreams she'd have.

Palaces, servants, money.

She opened her eyes. "Those really are dreams. Ones I might as well get out of my subconscious right now. Women like me don't belong in dreams like that."

Damien had made that clear.

She pushed up, held onto a nearby locker to get her bearings and reminded herself to get back to reality.

Her baby was still fatherless.

Two nurses came in and started to rifle through their lockers. Nola looked at her watch. Geez, she'd wasted the last hour of work.

It really was time to get back to normal, back to her plan. And, she thought, since she obviously didn't have the wherewithal to mentally avoid his trap, first on her list was sidestepping His Royal Intruder.

Nola pushed open the door to the OR suite and ran smack dab into Dr. Framer. "Excuse me, sir."

He gave her a fatherly smile. "No problem. I was coming to find you anyway."

"Oh?" This can't be good, she thought. The head of surgery wasn't searching her out to say goodbye for the day. "Is there something I can do–"

"Dr. Framer graciously invited me to dine at his home tonight, Nola, and he suggested you come along–to welcome me here," Del said from behind.

She leaned near Del. Through clenched teeth she muttered, "I'll just bet it was *his* idea." With a smile to Dr. Framer, she said, "I'm afraid I won't be able to–"

"Oh my," he said, then frowned. "I had already checked it with Ann. Your schedule is cleared of working the OR so that we can get the full benefit of His Highness's visit. Since you are in charge, I wanted you there, too. And my wife does love your company. She's planned a rather large dinner party."

His Royal Intruder observed smugly then turned toward the doctor. "Call me Del, please. No need for such formality."

She rolled her eyes and though of what else she'd like to call him.

Dr. Framer looked at Nola. "Perhaps whatever you had planned can be postponed?"

"Ally McBeal" isn't on every night, doc, she thought. "Oh gosh, I really don't think I can–"

Del leaned near. She could almost hear his mind churning out its devious thoughts. "Didn't you mention at lunch that you couldn't wait to get home just to *rest* tonight? Yes, I'm quite certain you didn't mention any plans."

Doctor Framer stood waiting, giving her a suspicious look.

Del leaned back so the doctor couldn't see him–then grinned.

Damn him. "What time is dinner, sir?"

"Seven."

"And–" Del opened his mouth. She gave him a look that would

76

silence the devil. "–*I'll* drive myself over."

Del's mouth shut.

"Well, but Del was telling me what a lovely tour you gave him today. The canyons are fabulous at sunset. You should show them to him–"

"Yes, sir, they are wonderful. But I need to drive myself. I just remembered I have a few errands to run. I'm certain His Highness has no need to see the inside of Soledad's only cleaners." She laughed.

Dr. Framer nodded, pressed the elevator button, and turned.

Before the doctor stepped into the elevator, Del said, "I've never been inside a cleaners–"

She pushed past him, poking the *close door* button before he could step in. "I'll certainly add As U Like It Cleaners to your tour someday, Your Highness."

His grinning face was the last thing she saw.

Damned, but he looked good.

Nola pulled into Dr. Framer's driveway. It looked like a used car lot of guests who earned over six figures, then there was her '95 Buick. A tiny space near the back of the drive was perfect. Out of the way so her poor car wouldn't feel slighted, and, more importantly, she could make a quick getaway after the meal.

She felt a migraine coming on. No wait, a stomach virus. Del couldn't follow her if she feigned a contagious illness since she'd insist she wouldn't want him to catch it. Even Dr. Framer couldn't interfere in that one–and she'd look heroic.

One of the anesthesiologists pulled in next to her. He'd only worked at St. Lucinda's about a month. He stepped out, looking darn good. The exact opposite of Del, this guy was blond as the sun, and several inches shorter. Still, he wasn't a turnoff. Hm, didn't she hear he was single? Maybe this dinner wasn't going to be a waste of time after all. No one said she had to sit with His Royal Intruder. She stepped out, rang the bell, and plastered on a smile.

The door opened. "How nice to see you, Nola," Mrs. Framer said, taking her arm. The hostess led Nola into the living room, which was full of formally dressed guests. She curled her lip so Mrs. Framer couldn't see and thought of how she'd rather be in her jeans. Thank goodness Holly had this spaghetti strapped number. Nola could have emptied her closet and never found a thing like this to wear. Mrs. Framer took her toward the dining room and pointed. "I've seated you next to our guest of honor since you know him the best."

In the biblical sense, Nola mused, but said, "Perhaps I should let someone else have the pleasure of his company since I do already—"

Del walked from behind. "How thoughtful of Mrs. Framer. I often times feel, well, a bit ill at ease in a foreign country. My accent and all—"

Mrs. Framer giggled like a teenager. The woman was sixty if she was a day.

Nola groaned. "Oh don't be silly. Your accent is adorable. I'm certain no one has a problem understanding you, Your Highness. Certainly one of the doctors would like to sit with you. With their penmanship, interpreting your accent shouldn't be a problem." She laughed.

Mrs. Framer stared at her. And Del nodded as if to say "touché." Then he forced a laugh. "I thought we could take this time to discuss my schedule."

"I'll discuss it all right," she muttered with a smile to the hostess and a jab to his side before heading into the room.

He was fast on her heals. "I bruise easily," he whispered near her ear.

For a moment she let the warmth of his breath tickle her skin. Then, thank goodness she had the wherewithal to step to the side. "In that case, Your Highness, you better stop trying to get us together before you have to change your country's colors to purple and green."

His hearty laugh filled the room.

"Stop it!" Several guests turned. Nola felt her face flush. "Stop that!"

"Keep it down, *chéri*."

"I said not to call me that," she whispered through clenched teeth while smiling to the other guests.

"Guess I am a creature of habit—"

"Habit isn't the word I'd use for the kind of creature you are."

Del laughed louder. The new anesthesiologist looked at them. Hm, he really wasn't bad. Was that a come-here smile? She'd actually never seen him without a mask on. Maybe now was the time she should go introduce herself. Yes. Yes, he was giving her an inviting look.

Then, he looked at Del, who had the craftiness to drape his arm around her shoulder at that very second! The guy was too much, she thought, while making a tight fist. The anesthesiologist turned to some nurse near him. Del was the beneficiary of Nola's fist.

"Ouch!" He glared at her. She tried to pull away, but he tightened his hold. "I know what is going on, but I also think you don't want to insult the good Dr. Framer by making a scene. We are sitting together, per Mrs. Framer's planning. Do you want to upset her, too?

"Of course not."

"And," He must have purposely breathed deeper because no one's breath came out *that* hot, "if you punch me like that again, *chéri*, I will have to remove you from the room–over my shoulder. Then deal with you in my own way."

He'd stressed the damned "*chéri*" part. Before she could say anything else, she felt someone come up from behind.

"Champagne?" a waiter took that opportunity to ask as he held out a silver tray laden with sparkling wine.

Del took one and handed it to her. She hesitated. He'd gotten her so riled she couldn't think of an excuse not to take it. She couldn't tell him that she didn't drink now–not after the gallons they'd shared in Mirabella.

"Thanks."

"You are welcome." He took a sip, watching her over the rim of the goblet. "And, I insist on calling you *chéri*."

She curled her lip at him, turned and smiled at one of the doctors on the other side of the room. "Come meet, Dr. Miller. He's the head of Orthopedics." With a smile, she let Del take the lead–as she leaned over and poured the champagne into Mrs. Framer's palm tree. Hopefully, it wouldn't kill it. She hated all this.

Del had her stooping to attempted murder of innocent plants.

Del shook Dr. Miller's hand, and before he could say a word,

Nola excused herself and left–make that sneaked away. He had to laugh at her spunky attempt, though, until he watched her head toward a rather nice looking man with golden hair. Earlier he'd looked in Del and Nola's direction, forcing Del to take her into his hold. Now she was smiling and talking to the guy, and Del was stuck here with Dr. Miller.

"So, Your Highness–"

"Call me Del, please." He forced a smile at Dr. Miller and watched Nola over the rim of his goblet. She was handing the guy some of the hors d'oeuvres. Del looked back to see Dr. Miller waiting, as if he'd asked him a question. "Sorry, sir. Did you say something?"

Dr. Miller gave him an odd look. "Yes, I asked when is the earliest that we'll see delivery of the orthopedic microscopes?"

"Microscopes?" He looked over the man's shoulder. She was having way too much fun. Dr. Miller cleared his throat. Del looked back. "Oh, yes, the microscopes. My factories are working overtime to fill the orders. I will let Dr. Framer know the exact–" She was heading out the back door! "–date. I...need some air. Please excuse me, sir."

"Certainly."

He was halfway across the room before he nodded to Dr. Miller. He stopped. Now he needed a reason to see where Nola headed. A waiter crossed the room with a tray laden with tiny lamb chops. Damn. She didn't eat lamb back in his country. But, wait! That would be a good excuse to engage her in conversation–even an argument. He reached up, took a fork from the tray and some lamb. Hurrying, he nearly knocked over a potted palm.

"Don't worry about the plant. The maid will clean it up," Mrs. Framer said, coming up from behind. "My, my, Your Highness, but you must be famished."

He looked at the four chops speared on his fork. "I...er...I seem to have misplaced Ms. St. Clair. I thought perhaps when I find her, she might be hungry." He stuck two on a napkin.

"Oh, my." Mrs. Framer's brow grew together. "I was quite certain she didn't eat meat last time we were at a hospital function. Of course, that was last year. I had the cook make her a special vegetarian meal–"

"Perhaps you are right." He shoved one chop into his mouth. Thank goodness they were boneless. "Why, yes. Now that you mention it." He ate one more.

"She's on the veranda with that nice new Dr. Tellgood."

"Veranda?"

"Porch, dear. It's a porch off the living room." She pointed to the left, leaned forward, her blue eyes mischievously sparkling and smiled. "Hurry. He is single, Your Highness."

Was that a wink? The observant woman must have been able to see the interest in his eyes. He bent, took her hand with his free one, and kissed it. She giggled. He excused himself.

Balancing the remaining lamb chops and his goblet, Del made his way out to the veranda, not certain about what he'd say, yet certain he needed to head out there.

Nola stood there laughing. The doctor looked mesmerized by her. Damn. The moon's glow highlighted her already fair skin. The dress she'd worn liberally allowed the silvery rays access to her skin. Thin straps no wider than a piece of string held the dress inches above her breasts. Were they fuller tonight? Yes, they looked–softer, larger. Oh, God. He grabbed so tight onto his napkin, one lamb chop flew off, landing on Nola's shoe. He bent, sending half a glass of champagne after the lamb.

"Look what you did!" She looked at him. Perhaps, he thought, "looked" is not the proper word. He knew the French term for her scowling face, but his English wasn't good enough to know the correct word to use to describe Nola right now. But what he could think of for the term did have something to do with "go-to-hell." He hurried forward, but before he could do the right thing to aid her, the fool doctor scooped the lamb off her shoe.

"Let me get a napkin, Nola," he said, turning to go.

"That's all right, Mark. I'm certain, His Royal–"

Del set his things on a nearby table. "How kind of you, sir. Please hurry so the stain does not set. Let me apologize, Nola–"

She drew her eyebrows together.

"That is not a flattering look for you, *chéri*."

She pushed past him to sit and take off her shoe. "How should I look when you throw lamb followed by champagne at me?"

He smiled. "I did not throw it. You know that. It was much like your olive and then there were the oranges—"

"I didn't *throw* olives and oranges at you." She paused. "Okay. You paid me back. Now beat it. Mark will be back with the—"

He stooped, took her ankle in his hold and wiped at her nylon with his linen handkerchief. "That, *chéri* —" He rubbed slowly, deliberately. "—is precisely why I am staying."

She yanked her foot away. With a motion swifter than the speed of light, she grabbed his handkerchief. "Beat it, Your Highness. I'm fine out here with Mark—"

"You call him so personally after merely knowing him a few minutes? I'd think you would use his last name. Call him 'doctor something.'"

She grabbed the lapels of his jacket and tugged him close. "It's a hell of a lot nicer name than I can think of for you."

She tugged so close, he could inhale her green apple shampoo. With a sigh, he cleared his thoughts, demanding he stay in control. "I know you are angry about the lamb—"

"You know I don't eat lamb anyway. What the hell possessed you to bring it out here?"

Del ran a finger up her leg, stopping inches below her knee. She hesitated before pulling it back. Hesitation, no matter how slight, was good, he told himself. Locking his gaze to hers, a feat he'd perfected with the women of the palace as a teen, he leaned closer. She pulled her legs together. He chuckled. "To answer your question, *you* possessed me to seek you out of all the guests and bring you a snack."

"Don't blame it on me—"

"Besides. The other day you insisted you are, and have always been a vegetarian. Then, in the Mexican restaurant you seemed...confused. Which is it?"

"My eating habits are none of your damn—"

"Um, excuse me. Here, Nola. I soaked this in club soda," Mark said, holding a paper towel toward her.

Del interceded. The towel tore as Nola yanked at her half. "Now look what you did."

"No problem, *chéri*." He took her shoe and the paper towel from her hand. Over his shoulder he said, "Thank you, doctor. Since the accident was my fault, I am obliged to take care of it. You may go."

Nola could only stare. It took minutes for her brain to unravel Del's actions.

Did he just have the audacity to dismiss Mark like some royal servant?

Chapter Seven

Nola yanked her shoe from Del's grasp. "You had no right to send Mark away. You treated him like your servant!" She tried to shove the stained shoe back on. The darn suede must have shrunk. "Of course something like that doesn't stop you. Oh, no–" She shoved harder. "–you do what you damn well please. Well that might work around your palace, but here is a different story. Quit sticking your nose in my business!"

While she ran her finger around the back edge to get the damp leather over her heel, she looked up. Del stood staring. Silently, he watched her every move. Pools of midnight sucked her under, swirling her thoughts. Her throat dried. Her heart fluttered. Her finger pinched between her heal and her shoe. And all with one look. She swallowed deeply, as if that would slice his gaze from her.

No chance.

He leaned against the wall overlooking the pool–and continued to stare. With his purposeful, enticing look, he spun a web of wanting like some poisonous spider–and captured her. It only took a few seconds. Now she knew how if felt to be paralyzed by some prey. All she could think was, there's no way to escape. With a final shove, the shoe finally covered her foot, but there was no hope in looking away.

Damn His Royal Intruder.

He didn't turn from her, merely walked slowly, deliberately, forward–never releasing her from his gaze.

All she could think to do was swallow again. How stupid, she thought. Turn, move, get the hell away from him!

But, she couldn't.

"Ah, but you accuse me unfairly, *chéri*. In my country, we believe in the cliché, all is fair in love and war. This is true in America. No?"

Nola sucked in enough air to swim the length of Dr. Framer's pool and back, twice. Bad move. Breathing so deeply with Del around was lethal. The night's breeze did its damnedest to carry his stupid cologne to her.

The web tightened.

"That...I mean...." Oh Great. What was she going to say?

"You mean what, *chéri*? Are you agreeing all is fair? That I can pursue, until you agree we belong together. That I am allowed to stick my nose–"

"Nose?" she murmured. The baby kicked. Nola's mind snapped to attention. Thank you, sweetie, she thought. Thank you for yanking Mommy back to reality. "No! I am not agreeing with you. And don't stick your perfect nose anywhere near me!" He grinned. She cursed. That "perfect" part wasn't meant to come out although he'd make an excellent model for a plastic surgeon's brochure even though his nose wasn't "store bought."

She stood, wiggled her foot inside her shoe until it fit better and straightened her frame. He remained a good foot taller. No matter. Height wasn't going to beat this guy–her brains would have to do. The feeling inside, though, reminded her that there was more to it than brains.

If only she could leave her heart out of this.

"All is *not* fair where feelings are concerned. I am single, over twenty-one, free to talk to, laugh with, or eat hors d'oeuvres with whomever I choose." He ran his slippery gaze down her dress. "You, on the other hand, have no right to interfere." She yanked her dress down as far as it would go.

Wearing the black revealing outfit was in fact a bad move. This was the last time she'd borrow anything from Holly. "Isn't ruining my wedding enough for you?" She looked to see several inches of skin still showed above her knees. Holly should get her money back for this outfit. Who said it was a dress? More like a slip–a teeny one.

"I told you, I'd do it again."

He'd made his way dangerously closer still, she realized, furious that she hadn't noticed him approaching. He'd gotten her thoughts so tangled, she couldn't think straight and certainly couldn't see straight. With a brush of his shoulder against her bare arm, he leaned near to whisper, "And again, and again if need be."

With a flip of her finger, she shoved some of her hair in front of her ear, wishing the feathery strands would drown out his voice. It was either that or go with the urge to tenderly touch the spot his breath heated. "Next...next time I'll elope. You'll never find me–"

His laughter rode the night's breeze much like his scent. "I have the means to find...."

She knew he was talking, but all she could think of was that he had the means for that and much more. Like taking away their child if he ever found out about it. "I'll manage somehow so you'll never know–"

His laughed died down. He leaned near and whispered, "Besides, *chéri*, I will not *allow* there to be a next time."

She had to get out of here. As much as she hated to admit it–she was no match for His Royal Intruder.

But she'd be damned if she'd give up trying.

She had to get away right now though to clear the cobwebs he'd spun in her head. Once alone and thinking straight, she'd plan things out better.

A waiter came out the door at the same moment she reached for the handle. That had to be some kind of divine intervention to aid her. "Dinner will be served in one hour, ma'am, sir," he said, turned and headed back inside.

Nola gave a scathing look to Del. "I don't think I could eat a thing thanks to your shenanigans."

"What are–"

She blew out a loud breath. "Oh, brother. Interference. Shenanigans are your interfering actions."

"Why would that cause you not to eat, *chéri?*"

Because I'd be next to you, inhaling, noticing, she thought, but she lied, "I...my stomach really doesn't feel that great."

He grabbed onto her arm. "I shall take you home."

"No, you shall not." Geez, she should have thought of another lie. Although she tried to scoot away, he didn't let go. With a firmness that wasn't painful, but certainly made her aware, he guided her toward the door.

"Whatever you wish. If you feel ill again, though, I'm taking you to the doctor."

Nola froze. What if he mentioned her "stomach" problems to one of the doctors! Surely the hospital grapevine had gone into full bloom once she'd announced her wedding. Every employee at St. Lucinda's must know by now that the said wedding was ruined, too. Oh geez, someone would be sure to tell him the cause of her stomach ailments.

She blew out a breath. "You know, all of a sudden I feel much better. Actually, I think I'm just hungry. And," she said with as much force as she could muster, "I wouldn't let you take me to the doctors anyway. If I was sick, drawing my last breath, I'd crawl on my hands and knees if need be. But, I would take *myself*."

He looked at her, and flashed his pearly whites.

Nola grabbed a stuffed shrimp appetizer from a wondering waiter's tray on her way in the door. Thank goodness His Royal Intruder stayed outside. With a shiver down her back, she likened him to a shadow. An annoying shadow. How the heck did Peter Pan manage to lose his shadow? If she remembered, she'd sever her unwanted royal shadow and no way would she sew it back on. She paused and shook her head. Now she was thinking in terms of fairytales. Del had her going nuts. Well, she decided, she wouldn't think of shadows or princes or her loss of sanity for at least a good hour.

She needed to concentrate on husband hunting.

Scanning the room, she looked for a sparkle of gold on each man's finger. Of course, in this day and age no ring was no guarantee that a man wasn't married. Across the crowd stood a man who met her gaze. She smiled. He nodded. That had to be a come-on. Nonchalantly she glanced at his finger. No golden glow. He must be the inhalation therapist who moonlighted at St. Lucinda's and lived in Albuquerque.

Okay, he'd do for starters.

With the shrimp resting on her bottom lip, she told herself this could be fun. And, it was necessary. The shrimp popped into her mouth, she wiped her hands on a napkin, shoved it onto a nearby tray and went in for the kill.

"Hi," she managed after the shrimp made its way down her throat.

He gave her the once over. She could feel his glance running up her body, and it wasn't what she expected or wanted. This was too painful. Making herself available was no fun at all. Actually, she felt like the poor shrimp she'd devoured; only this guy's gaze was devouring her chest at the moment.

"Nola isn't it?" he asked, getting a bit too close and smelling a lot like champagne.

Looser. "Yes. Please excuse me." She decided to fish around the room a bit more. When she turned, he grabbed onto her arm way too tightly. "Hey!"

"Wait a minute, baby. You came over here. Don't flash that chest at me and run off." His grip tightened. "I hear you're available now after some jerk crashed your wedding." He exhaled too close. She swallowed a gag.

Her heart started to race although she knew he wouldn't try anything in front of all these people. Obviously she didn't know much about slimy therapists, she thought, as he snaked his hand around and pinched her bottom.

She tried to swing her arm around to knock his away, but before she made contact, she watched his arm move back–gripped firmly by a golden tanned hand, a familiar ring reflecting the light. The guy's drink went sailing out of his hand, landing on poor Dr. Mumfred's tux. The elderly orthopedist, obviously taken by surprise, looked as shocked as Nola felt.

She turned toward Del. "Look what you did!"

He'd already started wiping Dr. Mumfred's jacket with his linen handkerchief. The hand-embroidered Dupre crest glared at her as he apologized to the doctor. In the mean time, the therapist had slithered away.

Del wiped faster. "I came to save you–"

"Save me! I can take care of myself!" She grabbed a napkin from the bar and started to wipe Dr. Mumfred's sleeve. "You've got a heck of a nerve, Your Highness."

"It's all right," the older gentleman said.

"No problem, sir." Nola wiped harder. "First the lamb, then champagne on my shoe, and now this."

Del ignored the doctor's insisting and ran the handkerchief over his lapel–all the while glaring at Nola. "If I hadn't come along to a save you, who knows what that jerk would have done?"

"Don't worry, you two. I'll have my wife send my tux to the cleaners," the doctor said, waving his hand about.

Nola curled her lip at Del and wiped more. "His Highness will be glad to pay–"

"Of course I will–"

Dr. Mumfred's grasp, amazingly strong for an older man, locked onto hers and Del's wrists at the same time. "I'm fine. Go enjoy your dinner. Seems you two lovebirds need to iron out something. Talk about whatever it is." With that, he made a quick getaway, leaving Nola sputtering a correction–and Del laughing hysterically.

Once the entire room had focused on them, she knew her pickens would be slim tonight.

"Damn, you, you Royal Intruder," she said through clenched teeth, turned and headed for the dining room.

He laughed louder.

Once in the dining room, Del sat down next to Nola. She'd busied herself talking to the man on her right obviously trying to ignore Del. Thank goodness the gentleman looked old enough to be her father, and thank goodness it wasn't Dr. Mumfred. Jealously had Del nodding to the man as he lifted his napkin, yet keeping an open ear as he covered the fine linen over his lap.

His plan was not going well, he thought.

Before he'd arrived to stop her wedding, he'd had the entire scenario plotted out perfectly. Henri had aided with his brilliance for detail, all the while keeping Del's thoughts logical.

How many hours had they spent on their scheme? How many times did the trusted Henri tactfully advise Del to think with his head and not his heart? He shook his head and sighed.

What could one do when love blinded them so?

He'd had his share of romances, but no one had come close to his Nola. Even the most beautiful, the shapeliest, those born of royalty could come close to the woman sitting next to him–trying her damnedest to avoid him.

He turned in time to see her reach for a roll. She laughed softly as if finding no humor in what the elder gentleman said, yet being polite.

He and his Magnolia should be on a plane back to Mirabella for their wedding. But, here they sat, her trying to avoid him, him trying to win her over.

He needed to call Henri tonight and re-adjust the fool plan.

Right now, thought, he'd "wing it" as the Americans say.

"Excuse me, *chéri*, could you please pass the butter? That is, if you are finished with it," Del said, smiling. "Oh, that's right. Excuse me. If I remember correctly, you do not intend to ever eat the stuff." Was that a growl much like a female tigress? At least he got a rise out of her.

She turned toward him. By the way she rubbed at her neck, trying to avoid him by spending the night talking to the gentleman next to her had given her a neck ache. How he'd like to ease the discomfort. She grabbed the butter dish so fast, the stick slid to the side.

"Look what you made me do."

He took his knife and gently pushed the butter back. The man, obviously feeling there was something going on that he didn't understand, turned toward the woman on his right. Del smiled. "I merely asked you to pass the butter."

She looked at his dish. "You don't even have any bread. I know what you are doing, Del. And stop it," she said under her breath, yet her words were very effective.

He took a roll from the basket in front of her while she still held the butter dish. "There. Now I have a roll. Please hand me the butter."

With a smile that made her eyes squint, she leaned near. "I'd like to take this butter and smear it over your–"

"Body?"

"Don't you wish."

"Yes, *chéri*," he whispered near her ear, "I most certainly wish exactly that you would smear the butter over my hot body."

Nola shoved the butter dish into his hand. How could two words sound so sensual? A momentary vision of rubbing butter across his chest, his abdomen, his.... Oh, God, she was loosing it. The man not only could read minds, it seemed he had a damn good power to control them, too.

"Is this seat taken?" Mark asked from across the table.

Thank goodness, she thought. Now she could at least have a decent meal and a chance at furthering her plan with the good doctor

91

since the rest of the guests most likely thought she was nuts–or worse yet, here with Del. Turning away to ignore His Royal Intruder, she smiled at Mark. "I don't believe it is–"

"And I believe our hostess has assigned all the seats," Del interrupted.

She kicked his leg under the table. "No. No, I am quiet certain she only put us together." Quickly smiling at Mark, she added, "Purely for business reasons."

Mark pulled out the chair and started to sit. "Then I won't be intruding?"

"Of course not, Mark."

"I'm afraid you will, sir."

"No, *Your Highness*, we can discuss what little business we have later tonight–"

"Ah, you are quite naughty, *chéri*." Del stuck his arm around her and nuzzled her ear! "Correct, Nola. Later tonight we will have plenty of time to discuss business...or whatever our heart's desire. Perhaps we won't *discuss* anything."

The guy was too much! She shoved his arm off. "My heart desires to eat in peace and go home–alone. And I am not, nor will I ever be *your* Nola!" She looked up to see Mark staring at her.

Oh great, she'd ruined her chance with this one, too.

No, she corrected, Del ruined it.

The rest of the meal passed in silence. Not that Del didn't make oodles of attempts at a conversation, but she managed to ignore him. That, she accomplished by not looking at him. Earlier, Mark had made an excuse to change his seat. She glanced at the end of the table to see him smiling at Helen Carpenter, a surgical nurse.

No great surprise. Helen was a recent divorcée with a somewhat "eager" interest in men. She'd be doing more than discussing business with Mark tonight. Another one out of contention.

The waitress handed Nola a dish of vanilla ice cream bathed in crème de menthe. "Could I please have it without the liquor?" Nola asked.

"Certainly, ma'am." She went to lift the dish. Del touched her hand.

"Why?" he asked, turning to Nola.

"Let her go, Del. I don't like mint."

The waitress looked at him. "To each his own."

He gave her one of his winning smiles, released his hold. The fool waitress giggled all the way out of the dining room, constantly turning around and ogling him. Then, he leaned toward Nola. "It does not make sense to me. You love mint."

"No I–"

"You have not forgotten how we fed each other those 'fabulous mints,' you'd called them, which my father had imported from Switzerland, after we–"

Made love, she thought. "That doesn't mean I want mint on my ice cream, Sherlock. Stop trying to interrogate me over stupid things like liquor on my ice cream." How she hoped he'd drop it.

No great surprise, he continued with, "You do remember eating the 'fabulous mints' don't you, *chéri?*"

"I also remember getting the chicken pox as a kid, my first cavity, getting a D in math, but that doesn't change the fact that I want my ice cream plain." She couldn't keep this up. He'd tried her patience throughout the entire night.

It was starting to hurt too much to continue.

Her heart wanted to tell him everything. How she felt. About the baby. Yet, her mind told her she couldn't. There was, after all, his country to think about, too.

"I have a headache," she lied, deciding she couldn't use the stomach virus line with his preoccupation with her bout of nausea the other day.

Del rose. "Let me take you home."

"No, Del. I am not incapacitated. I can drive myself home. I'll see you at work on Monday." She stood, turned and said over he shoulder so that only he could hear. "Do not follow me. Do not come by to check on me. And *do not* call."

"But, *chéri*–"

"I'll notify the superintendent to call you if I pass away in my sleep." With that, she turned and didn't look back.

If she did, she'd never leave.

Nola leaned back in the nurse's lounge couch for a few minutes.

Her head hurt since, needless to say, she hadn't slept well after the stupid dinner party last night.

His Royal Intruder was becoming a royal pain in the—

"Hey, Nola. There's some gorgeous guy out in the hallway looking for you," one of the OR nurses said. "Oh, wait. Isn't he that prince that is giving the inservice tomorrow?"

Nola pushed herself up. "I'm afraid so."

"Afraid? Why's that? I mean I was going to ask if I could take a picture of him to hang inside my locker. You know, like a pinup. I've never seen such dark hair." She purred.

Nola curled her lip. "I don't think that would be appropriate." Although not a bad idea if she had a set of darts. She smiled to the foolish nurse and pushed open the door.

And had to grab onto the wall.

"You didn't call me to discuss our schedule," Del said. He'd worn navy slacks today and what had to be a camel colored cashmere sweater. She'd never owned cashmere. Probably couldn't afford camel for that matter. He looked too good to be real, but she knew by her past memories that he sure as heck was.

"Sorry. Let's go downstairs. I'll show you where we'll set you up." She turned and walked in front of him, wishing she hadn't. How could him walking behind make her feel as if he was staring at her—and she could feel his stare on her back, her neck, and her bottom?

Man, they keep this hospital way too hot.

Wiping at her forehead, yet not feeling a drop, she decided they better use the stairs. No way did she want to get on the elevator with—

Closed for cleaning.

She looked at the yellow plastic sign in the doorway of the stairwell as if she couldn't read English.

"Is there an elevator nearby, *chéri*?"

"Of course." But I'd rather walk down wet stairs then get on with you. Then she thought of a possible fall again. "It's around the corner. Come on."

"Why so silent this morning?"

She couldn't tell him that she'd tossed and turned last night until a vision of his face was the last thing she remembered, until waking this morning. "I have a lot on my mind."

He gave her that tiresome concerned look. If he brought up her stomach again, she would get sick. The thought of diverting his attention away from her health never left her mind though each time the baby kicked. "With your visit. You know, I have a lot of planning to do."

"I see." He squinted at her as if not believing a word she said. Well, he could believe what he wanted, she thought as the elevator door opened. Nola hesitated. She looked around to see if anyone else might be coming to use the elevator. A nurse's aid wheeled a gurney down the hall. Yes!

Del stepped inside, holding the door with his foot. "Nola?"

"Hold it. That aid is coming, too." Nola stepped to the back, breathed a sigh of relief, and watched the aid wheel past the elevator!

Del released his foot. The door closed. She pushed against the back wall–and cursed.

In the above mirror, she noticed him grin.

If this thing stopped mid-floors, she'd...she couldn't even think of what she'd do. Passing out was her first choice but that wouldn't be good for the baby.

Del turned around. "You are looking pale, almost frightened." He touched her arm.

She brushed his hand away. "I'm fine. Keep your hands to yourself."

He stepped closer. And chuckled. "I have always been a good judge of character, and body language, Nola. You do not like being alone with me–yet months ago you cried out in joy during our love making."

"Too much Mirabellan champagne."

He smiled, ran a single finger along her arm. Why hadn't she worn her lab coat? Momentary paralysis had her arm stay put–directly under his touch.

How could one elevator ride take so long? She looked at the lights to make sure the think was moving to different floors.

"I'd hate to think those sounds of pleasure were liquor induced."

He leaned near, smelling terrific.

Her back hurt as she pushed further against the railing of the back wall. Open, door. Please. She wanted to say the liquor had in fact caused her reaction to him, but looking into the depths of his eyes–that was one lie that wouldn't come out.

His net captured her once again.

The elevator door opened. Nola realized she'd been holding her breath. Blowing out loudly, she hurried out, the prince close behind.

She caught his reflection in a nearby metal cabinet. Damn if he wasn't grinning. How she hated the reaction he'd caused–and she allowed herself to feel.

"This is where you'll give your inservice," she said as she opened the door to the amphitheater. Of course, he followed close behind. Her shadow.

Del looked across the large room, never taking his eyes off her. "This will be fine. Now, where can we set up a work area for me?"

"There's a small office down there." He followed her pointing, still smiling to himself inside. Even her finger shook. It wasn't that he wanted to make her feel uncomfortable, no way would he want that. It was just that her nervousness on the elevator and her actions now restored his hope.

She cared for him enough not to trust herself to be alone with him in the elevator. That made him happy. "Let's take a look at the office. I have several pieces of equipment I'd like to set up while I'm here. Various computers to show the doctors my equipment."

Nola started down the stairs of the amphitheater. "Fine. I'll have someone bring them here for you. Are they in your car?"

"Yes. That would be great." He hurried his step as she nearly ran down the stairs. She was making this all so very difficult.

But he relished the challenge–and the reward.

He'd never consider himself an arrogant man, he left that up to Damien. But Del felt so certain that Nola hid her true feelings for him, he knew he had to persist.

"What is so funny?"

"Hm?" He looked up. They were at the bottom of the stairs, she glaring at him, him off in his thoughts, smiling. "Well, *cheri*, I was thinking of us–"

"There is no us. Unless you mean the "us" who is working together until you leave." She leaned near. "When is that, by the way?"

"I told you as long as it takes."

"That's right. I guess when you are a prince you can make your own rules."

How he wished that was true, but it wasn't. "Actually, there is an 'us' no matter how much you deny it. And, I don't make the rules of my country, but I–" He couldn't help himself. He took her into his arms. Thank goodness his surprise had her unable to move. Her body softened in his hold, a look of desire in her eyes. With a brush of his lips over hers, he whispered, "–will remain in the United States until you agree to come back with me."

The glassy look in her eyes disappeared. She pushed at his chest, walked across the stage and over her shoulder said, "Then I hope you have a very long lease on your sublet. A hundred years should do it."

He laughed and followed her toward a door. She opened it and stepped inside. "It's not huge, but will suffice for your *brief* stay."

Eager to get his work accomplished so he could fully concentrate on Nola, he looked around. "It'll be fine. And–" Leaning so near he could inhale her green apple shampoo, he finished with, "–I intend to make my stay brief."

"You...I." She pushed him away. He heard her take a breath and say, "I'll go have your stuff brought in."

Del leaned against the wall and smiled. "I will be waiting for you–."

She walked out, slamming the door behind her.

"–for as long as it takes for you to admit your love, Magnolia."

He looked at the monitor on his watch. Hopefully I *won't* run out of time.

Chapter Eight

Nola flipped the power switch. Del's computers and various other pieces of electrical equipment whirred alive in the tiny office she'd set up. With a cleaver twist of fate, she'd found a new doctor to introduce Del to so he could observe surgery and now had a few minutes of peace without him around. The last of the orderlies set the final box on the table and asked, "Anything else, Ms. St. Clair?"

"No, Bob, thanks. I can take it from here."

He looked around the room. "Looks like some kind of command center with all this equipment."

She chuckled. "It does. Mirabella is quite the leader in technology–"

"And we've worked very hard to get there," said Henri's disembodied voice.

"Shoot!" Bob jumped. "Where'd that come from? "Who's that?"

"Hank. I mean Henri, personal assistant to the prince. Where the heck are you–" She turned to see the smiling face of Del's assistant on the monitor behind her.

Bob gave a nervous wave, "I'm outta here," he mumbled, scurrying out the door.

"I'm afraid you scared one of the orderlies, Hank." She laughed and walked closer.

"Orderlies, *Mademoiselle*?"

She sat on a chair and wheeled in front of Henri's screen. "This is too cool. Oh, orderlies are male helpers around the hospital. This screen is so clear. Like you are really here." With a finger she touched at his nose. "You feel that?"

"No." His face grew ruddy.

"Maybe you can work on that next. Touch vision."

He chuckled. "I'll pass that along to our engineers."

She had the strange urge to hug the screen. He'd become such a good friend to her in Mirabella. Henri had been her savior when Damien had.... None of that, she told herself, smiling at Henri. It was just that the portly man was so huggable. "So, what brings you to the screen, Hank. Getting tired of popping up on Del's watch? If that's the case, can't say's I blame you." She smiled. Henri cleared his throat. "If you get any redder, Hank, I'm going to have to adjust the

99

tint on this screen."

He chuckled. "Actually, His Highness isn't expecting me–and no need to tell him we spoke."

Hm. "Secrets. You got a secret for me, Hank? Ooooh, I love that!"

"No, *Mademoiselle*, I do not, nor would I keep secrets from His Highness."

"Okay. Okay. I understand your allegiance to him. It's great to be so dedicated. So you materialized just to see me? Great. What's going on back there?"

For a second, she thought she noted a glimmer of concern in the man's clear blue eyes. Maybe the screen's reception wasn't that good. Then he gave her a wide smile and said, "We are keeping quite busy here as usual."

"How's the king?"

"The king?" Odd the way he asked that. "Why of course he is fine...the same."

Nola leaned near, resting her arms on her elbows, chin in her palms. If the king were fine why did Henri seem so nervous? "You sure?"

"Of course."

"Good. Good. Give him my regards."

"I shall. He was very taken in by you. I'm quite certain he would love to see you again. He had mentioned you quite often after you'd...er...left so abruptly."

So the king had noticed, too. "That's nice, but–"

"Perhaps you will visit soon?"

Was there a devious look in the man's eyes? She wasn't sure, nor could she tell him she had no intention of ever going back to his country, so she evaded that issue. "Guess there's no need to ask about the queen. I'm sure she wouldn't love to see me again." She laughed.

Henri looked embarrassed, but said, "Her Royal Highness is...rather set in her opinions. She did find you–"

"Nuts?" They both laughed.

"No, *Mademoiselle* Nola, you are not how you say 'nuts.' You are the most delightful woman Prince Delmar has ever met."

Nola straightened up. No way did she want to get into a discussion about Del or his women. "Well." She sighed. "I should get back to work before Prince Delmar fires me–"

"You've changed him, Nola," he said softly as if knowing full well he had no right to speak for the prince–yet also knowing he had to.

Oh God, how could she let that one pass? She should poke the Off button, sending Henri into the depths of technology. But her finger paused near the switch. She wiggled it, then hesitated. Her finger shook as Henri waited silently. "How so, Henri?" she said softly.

"Prior to meeting you, His Highness was most serious. He paid too much attention to the country's needs–instead of his own. Do not misunderstand, *Mademoiselle*, he is a genius in business. I would never question his dedication to Mirabella either. But, when you came...I have said far too much." He shut his eyes for a moment.

When he opened them, Nola felt an emptiness deep inside. Even the baby lay silent. She should have stopped Henri earlier, but foolishly, or maybe selfishly, she wanted to hear what he had to say.

Now she wished she could turn back time.

Turn it back to ten minutes ago.

Or, she admitted, turn it back to four and a half months ago–when she would never have allowed herself to fall for the prince–knowing today's outcome.

She smiled to the screen. "I really have to go, Hank. Nice talking to you." As she pushed the button, she heard a faint, "Please give him...."

She shoved at the button to turn it back on. Give him what? The screen crackled, remained blank. Maybe Henri had turned off something on his end. Now she wouldn't know what he was going to say. Damn it. It'd eat away at her no doubt, but she refused to ask Del how to contact Henri because, with the way Del had been lately, he'd probably read her mind and find out why she wanted to.

She swung the chair around several times, mumbling, "Give him what? Your time? Your patience? Your lifesaving's? Give him your–" Del stood in the doorway, grinning. Thank God she'd caught herself before she said, "*Heart.*"

Grabbing onto the desk before the spinning made her nauseous, she realized just how good she felt lately. Come to think of it, she'd been feeling great. Maybe this middle trimester was going to be a breeze. She looked up into Del's eyes and thought, she may be feeling wonderful physically, but mentally she was a wreck.

"You have done a fine job with everything, Nola. Sorry I couldn't be around to help." He crossed the room, adjusting a few cables on the way.

"No problem." She stood, held onto the table a second and forced a smile. "How'd the surgery go?"

He raised an eyebrow as if he thought her nuts, too. "I was only there to observe the microscope working. You make it sound as if I performed it."

"Oh, yeah. Silly me." There went her brain. All he had to do was come into the room and she fell off her "logic" wagon. Darn the conversation with ole Henri, too. He'd started her out feeling so confused. She'd have to be wearier of him. Seems he had something up his sleeve where the prince was concerned. That's all she needed. A meddling assistant whose dedication rivaled The President's Secret Service.

Well, at least she could switch off Henri into oblivion. Del was another matter. Footsteps made her look up. He'd come uncomfortably close. Once again she'd drifted off in thought while he moved in for the kill. She told herself to play it cool. Keep her head. Don't let her hormones rule–make her do what she *never* should.

He touched her arm, gently.

She tried to take a step back, but her body once again did its own thing. Looking up, she found herself inches from Del's face, her arms around his neck, and seconds away from disaster.

"There's nothing silly about this, *chéri*."

Oh geez! He'd whispered the words so very near her ear, his breath sent her hair to tickling her cheek. She blinked. No luck. She was still in his arms. As a matter of fact, he'd taken her position as some kind of come-on and leaned closer. "No, Del...." *Don't kiss me.* The last words stayed a thought–he kissed her.

Del couldn't believe the luck that landed Nola in his arms like this. He ran his lips across hers gently at first incase she pulled back. But he needed to be cautious, he thought as her breasts pressed into his chest. The tips stiffened against his shirt. Signals bombarded his brain as if electric currents rained from the computers. But he knew the real cause that hardened him against her thighs–and the world seemed a wonderful place.

He couldn't help pull her closer, kiss her deeper. "Does this make you feel good, *chéri?*"

"Um..."

He held her back a second to see the sparkle of her eyes, hear her soft breaths and inhale green apple. Running a finger across the silken skin of her cheek, he chuckled. "I'm so very glad."

"Very glad," she murmured.

Nola felt his chuckle against her cheek before she realized that she'd lost her mind. His hold, his touch, the kisses he ran along her throat, behind her ear, to the nape of her neck and back made certain she'd never be able to think logically again.

But who cared?

Dizziness that she'd felt days ago surfaced in his touch, but this time she welcomed the heady feeling. If she faltered, he'd catch her in his strong hold. If she stumbled into his solid chest, she'd feel secure. And if she all out fainted from his effects–she'd surely wake with a smile on her face.

Warm words heated her cheek as he said under his breath, "I want to make you feel heavenly, *chéri.*"

"You're doing a good job...."

He lifted her blouse enough to sneak his hands beneath. The room's air-cooled her skin as currents swirled beneath the fabric. He worked his tender touch to the soft mounds that grew fuller each day. Heat from deep inside seared through her. At any moment he'd burn his fingers on her skin.

"I want to make you weaken in my hold until you beg me to take to you to our special place. The place we'd once shared. Give me your–"

Del felt the pressure before he knew what had happened. She'd pushed so hard when his mind was on other things, Nola landed him against the table. "What's that about?"

103

He yanked at her blouse. "I...I'm not giving you anything except my time here at work. You had no right to force me–"

He flew from the table, landing inches from her face. "Do not ever accuse me falsely."

"I didn't mean to–"

"When are you going to admit the truth to yourself, Nola? You act as though our actions are all one-sided. They are not. I forced nothing."

"I–" He was right, she knew. There was no way he'd forced any of this on her. She'd welcomed it, craved it since the day he'd stopped her wedding, but no way would she admit it. His face wrinkled in anger. "I'm sorry. Please calm down." It wasn't fair to lead him on–make him angry. She knew that, but it was so hard to stop him once he started looking at her with those eyes, coming closer, or kissing her. "Look. I'm not thinking clearly right now."

His face softened. He grinned. "I have that effect on you, yet you deny it."

"No you...stop confusing me."

He wanted to grab her again, but knew the force would be excessive. She'd deepened his wound with her accusation. He could only take so much. All along he'd been patient, but he knew himself to be a man–not a saint. "The intention is not to confuse you, *chéri*. More for you to admit...the truth. I want you to give me your–

"Stop that! First Henri. Now you–" Her hand flew to cover her mouth.

Del glared at her. "What does my assistant have to do with this?"

She bit at her lip. "Nothing."

He moved disturbingly close. "Why mention him?"

"I don't know. It slipped out. I guess." She tried to turn from his gaze but had no luck.

"Odd that Henri would pop into your mind like that."

One more step forward. That did it. She looked him in the eye and could only say, "Well, it's just that...Henri called on that." She pointed.

His eyes widened, breaking the mood. He turned to look at the screen behind him. "When? What did he say?" He grabbed onto Nola's shoulders. "Is everything all–" Fear covered her eyes. What was he doing? If there was an emergency at the palace, Henri would have called him on his watch. Del was much too sensitive to his father's troubles. He let her go.

Now she did it, Nola thought. She'd broken her trust with Henri. Damn Del and his stupid kisses, stupid eyes, stupid body that he'd pressed against her–reminding her what she could have–what she *wanted.* "Let's go over the schedule–"

"Later. Excuse me." He turned on the screen and dialed a zero.

Nola felt her heart sink. With that, she moved to the door. "When you're finished, I'll be in the cafeteria. It's past lunch," she muttered.

Del nodded. Before she opened the door, Henri appeared a bit fuzzy on the screen, yet no doubt looking from Del, directly to her.

She grabbed the handle, hurried out and shut the door not able to look Henri in the face. Making her way to the cafeteria, she knew this was going to be one of those meals where she'd have to shove down every bite. Her stomach told her she was hungry, needed nourishment for the baby, yet her mouth said it was going to be as dry as the desert out past the canyons.

Thank goodness the lunch line was short, because she needed to sit down soon. Her feelings were so jumbled, she thought she might explode. First the confusing conversation with Henri, then the kiss, then the argument. Darn but she'd run the spectrum of feelings this time.

She grabbed a salad, ordered the turkey dinner and poured herself a glass of water. Right now she couldn't even force a glass of milk down if she tried. She faithfully took her prenatal vitamins, so missing a few drinks of calcium wouldn't hurt.

Across the cafeteria she saw Holly walking out the door. Good. No way did she feel like explaining why she looked such a mess, as she surely must. The cafeteria lady had given her a look that said she did. Holly, although a dear friend, would only make Nola feel worse.

The fool would chastise her for not giving into Del, not leaping at the chance to fly across the ocean at Henri's suggestion and...well, she wouldn't go into any details about the kiss.

There was no doubt in her mind what Holly would have said about that.

And, she sighed, she wouldn't have any ammo to argue against that one.

After a sip of water, she decided she needed to get this job done in record time and Del out of her life. It wasn't going to be easy, but– Geez. She didn't have a "but." Every cell in her body rebelled against her logic.

Until the baby kicked.

It always did during a meal or shortly after. The not so gentle reminder of a foot or fist against her inside reminded her that the only one she could think about right now was her baby. If Del ever found out, she had no idea what lengths he would go to and cause her trouble.

After all, look at the damn command center he'd had her set up for him in only a few hours.

He had the means–and she wasn't sure of his motives.

Look how, in a flicker of a television screen, Henri could intrude into her life. And look at how in a moment of insanity, Del managed to kiss her–when she knew she shouldn't let him.

She blew out a breath and the lie that she didn't enjoy it.

While he finished his lunch, she'd write up a schedule that would send him into overdrive. At least if his inservices were completed, he couldn't be hanging around the hospital annoying her–enticing her. He'd have to go to the other hospitals out of dedication to his country's company.

So, she'd get him the heck out of Soledad that way.

"How's the turkey?" Del asked.

Nola's gaze flew up from her plate to see him standing over her table. Her hand started to shake. The way her knees felt under the table, if she stood, she knew she'd topple into his arms. And, the worse part was, if she spoke right now her voice would come out a throaty whisper.

She had to be more aware of him sneaking up on her so he wouldn't affect her like this. Nodding, she took a forkful of mashed potatoes.

"I'll take that as a positive food critique. Excuse me, *chéri*, while I get my meal."

"Take your time," she managed and decided she needed to eat

fast and leave. No one said she had to spend every waking hour with the man. She'd make an excuse to hightail it out of here as soon as he returned. Shoveling the food in, she watched him work his way down the lunch line. He was near the cashier, soon to be at the table. With one last spoonful to go, she decided to leave it and get out while she could. Whisking the napkin across her mouth, she shoved it onto her tray, stood and turned.

"Having a late lunch, Nola?" Ann Priner asked.

Geez, and she'd almost made a clean getaway. "Hi, Ann. Yeah, I'm kinda in a hurry." She smiled and turned to go.

"But, Nola, your prince is only getting his food now. Surely you aren't leaving him alone?"

Nola sank into her chair. "He is not *my* prince."

Ann gave her an odd look. "I only meant you're like an ambassador to Mirabella, representing our hospital–"

"Sorry, Ann. I'm not thinking clearly today."

Ann leaned near. "Everything all right with the baby?"

"Yes!" She swung around to see Del paying for his lunch. "No problem. Actually, I feel so good, I often forget. Seems if I'm reminded, I start feeling queasy."

Ann smiled. "Then I won't mention it again."

"Thanks. Ann? What's wrong?" She turned around to see what Ann was staring at. Oh, great.

"Hello, *Mademoiselle* Priner."

Nola groaned at Ann's glowing look. The woman was pathetic, nearly drooling over His Royal Intruder. Then again, she couldn't blame her, Nola admitted as she watched Del stand near his chair. She should have known he wouldn't sit down while Ann stood. Okay, she'd give him credit for impeccable manners. It was kind of nice to have a man act like that instead of, oh, pinching her bottom in public like the sleazy therapist.

"Sit down, Your Highness, before your food gets cold." Ann stood back and motioned toward the chair.

Del hesitated.

"For crying out loud, sit!" As soon as the words came out, Nola cringed. The reaction came naturally, then she saw the horrified look on her supervisor's face. Geez. Now she was in trouble at work because of him.

He must love this.

Del took her hand into his. "Thank you, Ms. St. Clair."

Both she and Ann stared at him as if he were nuts. His grip tightened as if reminding her to go along with whatever nonsense he was up to. "No problem," she muttered.

"You see, *Mademoiselle*, I asked Ms. St. Clair to treat me as one of the, how do you call them, 'the guys' while I am here. It makes me feel as if I belong better than being treated like some outsider."

"Heavens, Your Highness, we'd never consider you an outsider. More like a special guest. A royal visitor." Ann grinned like the Cheshire Cat.

Nola shook her head when Ann wasn't looking. "Well, I really need to get going. I'll meet you in the office, Del."

Ann raised an eyebrow. "Nola, you're certainly not going to let His Highness eat alone?"

Nola sank into the chair. "I'll keep you company–unless you want me to leave."

A twinkle flashed into his eyes as he said, "I would love your company, Ms. St. Clair."

She kicked his shin under the table. Luckily his reaction went unnoticed by Ann. She seemed satisfied as she said her good-byes and headed out of the cafeteria.

Del took a sip of his cola, leaned back in his chair, and looked at her.

"What?" Scrapping her chair on the floor, she shifted to the side.

"I'm waiting."

"For what?"

"You disappoint me, *chéri*. I saved your, how do you call it "butt" from getting into trouble with your boss and you don't thank me?"

She growled at him. "Eat." With that, she pushed his tray toward him, stuck her elbows on the table despite his we-don't-do-that-in-my-country look and rested her head in her palms. The man was exhausting.

The baby kicked, sending that warm maternal feeling throughout her. She peeked at Del as if expecting him to comment, to know that his child did somersaults inside her. She'd taken to wearing her most baggy tops and a lab coat was becoming a must.

Saddened that she couldn't share the joy, she shut her eyes for a few minutes. "Let me know when you are finished."

Del watched Nola as he ate his meal. She looked adorable as if trying to hide from him like some ostrich. "What are our plans after lunch?"

She lifted one eyelid. "Go over you schedule. Tomorrow you start your inservices. They'll run until Sunday."

"Sunday? I had no intention of giving any inservices over the weekend."

She opened her eyes, sat upright. "I...there is a lot to cover in a short time."

"No, the time won't include the weekend. I will not inconvenience the staff by having them give up their days off."

"How thoughtful." She curled her lip at him.

"Besides, I thought we could do something this weekend. Maybe get away. Have you show me around New Mexico."

"No! I mean I can't. I'm busy."

"You just said we were going to be working." He set down his fork, took a sip of cola and finished, "How can you be busy if I cancel the inservices?"

He had her there. "I do have a life outside the hospital you know."

"I'm certain you do. But, it sounds to me that it includes secluding yourself in your apartment. Holly said you never get away–"

"When did you talk to her?" The big mouth.

"In the hallway a few minutes ago." He wiped his napkin across his face. "I am finished. Shall we go?"

Nola hesitated, then stood. "Traitor," she whispered, but he'd heard. For some reason, Nola refused to leave town. She'd moved here, according to Holly, right after nursing school and never left. Odd, he thought, deciding he needed to find out why. Thank goodness, though, she at least left the one time to come to Mirabella.

Nola walked out of the cafeteria so quickly, Del had to return his tray and hurry to catch up with her. "So, I understand Carlsbad Caverns are interesting."

"I don't know. Never been...we have some small caverns right here in Soledad. I'll give you directions to them if you have a burning desire to explore underground."

He grabbed at her arm. "No, I don't. I merely wanted to spend some time with you away from this little town."

"I don't want to, Del."

"Why?" He took her by the shoulders and stopped her. "If you don't give me a better reason, I'll make a scene here. I'll try to get the truth from you in my own way."

"You wouldn't—"

He leaned downward, ready to kiss her. She pushed at his chest. He let go in time for her to scoot away. Following her down the hall, he nodded at several nurses who found their interaction something to stare at.

"Holly is exaggerating. She does that."

They'd made it back to the office. Nola sat in a chair and pulled out a file. "Here is the schedule." She handed a sheet of paper toward him. "This is your copy."

He took it and sat on the desk directly in front of her. She tried to wheel the chair to the side, but he stuck his knee in the way. "Why won't you leave this town? It's not normal to stay in one place and not see the world."

"Normal? What does someone who's never been to the cleaners or grocery store know about normal?"

"I didn't choose to be born into a royal family. So I don't have much choice in my daily life—you do. Yet you choose to stay here. And I want to know why."

She pushed at his knee. He held it firm. "Let me get up."

"Not until you give me a good reason."

When she looked up at him, he wished he hadn't persisted. A sadness dulled the beauty of her eyes. If he didn't know Nola to be such a strong woman, he'd wonder if it weren't tears glossing over the usual sparkle. He moved his leg. "I'm sorry, *chéri*. You don't need to tell me—"

"My mother was a teenager. Her mother an alcoholic who drank herself to death before I was three. So, not having any kind of decent role model, my dear mother chose to give me up for adoption at the

110

age of seven. I had no other relatives. Only thing is, most people, at least the ones in the boonies of Louisiana, wanted newborn babies. They didn't want–"

He lifted her from the seat, cradled her in his arms. And, thank the Lord, she let him. "I'm sorry–"

"Why should you be? It's not your fault that she didn't want her own daughter. You have no idea how it feels to have your mother give you up at that age–when you can remember. If she'd put me up for adoption when I was born, I'd know it was because she wanted what was best for me–that she loved me." She sucked in a breath. Del tightened his hold.

"She actually told me that she didn't love me. That I was a burden she was getting rid of. I spent the rest of my youth shifting from one foster home to the other. That's where I met Holly and Rusty. Only they both got adopted around the age of twelve when we lived at Miss Josie's. It only added to my feeling more unloved, more worthless–abandoned yet again."

"But you've made something of yourself."

She pushed away from him and walked to the window. "Yes, in Soledad. I'm accepted as everyone else." She turned to him. "You know, it killed me to go to Mirabella, but my boss at the time wasn't Ann. It was a man who I couldn't share my past with. He wouldn't have cared anyway. It was my only chance to keep my job. So, I went."

"I am so glad you did, *chéri*."

A pained look filled her eyes. "Unfortunately–I'm not."

Chapter Nine

Del watched Nola walk out of the office. He thought better than to go after her. Obviously she needed to be alone. It hurt that she refused his comfort, but he understood her pain. He'd give her some time then find her. Sinking into a chair, he leaned back and thought of his wonderful childhood. Anger that a mother could affect a child's life so thoughtlessly had him gripping the chair.

"Excuse me, Your Highness," Henri said.

Del spun around to see Henri on the screen. "I guessed you might be in your office–"

"What is it, Henri? Father?"

"I am afraid so. He is fine, but he wandered off the grounds last night–"

Del grabbed the monitor. "Why weren't you watching him?" He eased his grip when he noted the sorrow in his assistant's eyes. "I'm sorry, Henri. I know what a wonderful job you do. Excuse my anger. It comes from worry."

"*Oui*, Your Highness. I have never let the king out of my sight since you left...until last night. Damien–"

"No need to say more."

"But, Your Highness, he tricked me into thinking the king was asleep in his chambers. I myself had seen to his comfort. When I went to prepare for sleep in the adjacent room, your brother waited for me there. He...I am afraid he'd been drinking."

Del leaned back. "I suspected he overdid the champagne. What did he do?"

Del could see how difficult it was for his friend to continue. Henri wiped at his brow several times before saying, "Damien suspects."

"Damn him."

"He claimed he'd gone in to say good night to the king. Lately Damien has been around the palace more and more. I have seen him lurking near your father, whispering."

Del bit his lip. He had to or he'd loose control. Not at his trusted friend, but at his unscrupulous brother. Damien's own interest always came first. Even as a child, he abused his birthright, ordering servants to do his bidding, spending money as if there were an unending supply, and in his days at university, failing subjects while he partied instead. No wonder he and the queen got along so well. "Please try to do your best, as I know you always do, Henri, to keep him away from my father."

"I shall. He had woken up your father and left the door open. Before I enter into my bed each night, I make one final check on the king. Last night he was gone. I found him in the rose garden, singing."

"Does Damien know?"

"He had left the palace earlier. No one knows. On Monday Queen Francine left for Monaco."

"Good. And Prince Angelica?"

"Your brother's wife has gone with the queen."

"How long?"

"The queen does not share information with me. But, your father said two weeks."

"If we can believe him. Any word from the royal doctors?"

"They say they are completing their testing today. He is with them now or I would not be able to talk to you. Shortly they should have a diagnosis of the king's health."

"No one needs to tell us, Henri."

"*Oui.*"

"Still, keep the doctor's report private until I arrive. By then the cartel should have things settled, the contracts signed, and Damien will have no recourse. And hopefully we are wrong and Father can continue to rule."

"And your plan, how is it going, Your Highness?"

"Not well, I'm afraid."

Henri frowned. "Oh dear. You are following the plan? Not making a pest of yourself, yet being available for her to see the truth? Sometimes, begging your pardon, you can be a bit...determined."

"Don't nag, Henri."

"I mean that only in a good way."

Del chuckled at Henri's insulted look. "I'm teasing. Seems our plan needs a bit of updating."

"*Mademoiselle*, is not cooperating?"

Del laughed. "I'm lucky she doesn't have me arrested for stalking her. I follow her around like a puppy, yet each time she turns and snaps my nose with a newspaper."

Henri laughed, then grew serious. "Unfortunately, time may not be on your side." He sighed.

Del frowned. "I will do my best. You know, Henri, it is not as much fun to pursue as to be pursued."

Henri laughed. "I would not know."

Del shook his head. "Of course not, since you are a confirmed bachelor. Still, the queen's secretary can't take her eyes off of you."

Henri stuttered.

Del chuckled. "Well, I must be going to continue my pursuing. Good bye."

Henri nodded before the monitor went blank. Del touched the screen, feeling the warmth of his closest friend. He knew he would never trust anyone as much as he did Henri. Their relationship went back years to when Henri worked for the king. As a teen Del spent many days learning the business from Henri.

Although he loved his father dearly, the king had changed under Queen Francine's influence. Not that father was anything like her, but Del noticed her favoritism of Damien when they were teens with his father having less say where Damien was concerned. Henri became more of a confidant that an employee to Del since the king traveled so often or was busy with matters of the country.

Del chuckled, remembering the discussions he'd had with Henri about dating. He loved him like a second father. Right now, though, he needed to concentrate on getting things settled here so he could hurry back to Mirabella–to his first father.

He looked at his watch. That screen, too, remained blank as if telling him he was running out of time.

The door opened behind him. "We need to get working," Nola said.

Del spun around to see her standing in the doorway. She looked recovered, but he still wanted to run and take her into his arms. "Yes, we need to get to work so that I may return to my country."

Nola hesitated. That was odd him saying that. What a change. Something must be wrong at home. She had a feeling Del wasn't talking about any inservice though when he said they needed to get back to work. Or, maybe she was reading too much into his words. After all, she dreaded facing him since her earlier confession. One thing she did not want from him or anyone else for that matter was sympathy. Life dealt her some crummy cards, but she made the most of them.

Her only stipulation was that the cards be dealt to her here in Soledad.

"Come on. I have to introduce you to the rest of the surgeons."

He walked to her, stepping aside so that she could go first. "No way." She moved to the other side. "I want you in front this time."

He grinned. "You wound me, *chéri*."

She poked at his arm. "Go. We'll make a quick stop by the ER to heal your wound."

Del paused, turned and grabbed her by the arms. "Would that it were so easy."

With that he brushed his lips across hers before she could pull away. As soon as she did, she shouted, "Stop doing that!" then pushed his shoulder until he turned around. "Go down to the second floor."

Nola watched Del's shoulders shake with laughter as he walked in front of her. This was all so funny to him. Well, she didn't find his advances the least bit humorous. Before he turned the corner, her gaze was drawn to his butt. Why did all the best looking guys have such narrow hips, such tight buns?

She could feel her hips widening by the minute.

Del was right, though, they had to finish their work together so he could leave. Pretty soon she'd be out of baggy clothing to camouflage her growing waistline.

And out of self-control when it came to his butt.

He turned to her. "Shall we take the elevator this time?"

"Funny." She looked to see the stairwell had no cleaning sign. "You know I don't want to be secluded on an elevator with you."

He leaned near and grinned. "We are of differing opinions on that one."

She curled her lip. "Go down the stairs. Dr. Edward's office is to the left. Then we'll head to the orthopedic department. That should cover meeting all the doctors for you."

"What about Olie?"

Was that a twinkle in Del's eyes? Surely he couldn't suspect—Naw, she was way too sensitive about hiding her pregnancy. Trying to sound nonchalant, she said, "You already met him."

"I know, but we didn't discuss business."

Oh God, what *did* they discuss? "I'll tell him to come to the inservice." She pushed open the door to Dr. Edward's office and nodded toward the receptionist.

Del was close behind. When he smiled at the woman, she dropped the phone receiver. "Besides, surely there are other obstetricians at St. Lucinda's. I would like to meet them first," he said.

"Dr. Edwards is free now, Nola," the receptionist said. She picked up the receiver, tapped it against her chin all the while eating Del up with her gaze.

Nola shook her head. "Your other line is buzzing, Maurine." Leaning over so Del couldn't hear, she said, "I'll be in the OB clinic for a few minutes."

Oblivious to the woman's ogling, Del followed Nola to the inner offices. She left him there and walked to the OB clinic. What could she say to her doctor to keep him from spilling the beans about her condition?

"Thank goodness," Nola muttered as Sheila, the OB receptionist, informed her that two of the doctors were in surgery and the other had the afternoon off.

"Do you need to see someone? Jill, the nurse practitioner, is still here."

"No. No, I'm fine. It was business." She turned to leave. "Wait, Sheila, could I just speak to Jill for a minute?"

"Hang on. Let me see what she's doing." Sheila punched a number on the phone, then offered the receiver to Nola. "She's on the line."

Nola held the phone for a few seconds. She'd never been a very good liar. Too much punishment came one's way in foster care if you were labeled as a liar. She chose to tell the truth and let the chips fall. Right now, though, she didn't want any of them falling on her secret.

"Hello?"

"Oh, hey, Jill. Nola St. Clair here. I was wondering—"

"Everything all right?"

"Oh, yes. It's just work related—"

She could hear Jill purring on the other end of the line. "I saw your 'work related' prince. Man, what I'd give to be showing him around. He's so gorgeous. Looks like a Mirabellan version of Antonio Banderas." She laughed. "A real dream."

Nola forced herself to join in so as not to sound suspicious. "He's a dream all right." Nightmare, she corrected. "Look, Jill, with him being from a foreign country and all, I don't want him getting any ideas about single American woman."

"If I weren't married, I'd like to give him some ideas."

"You are too wicked." Stop being such a fool. "Anyway, could you spread the word to the staff here that my pregnancy better be hush-hush for the next few days?"

Jill hesitated. "I guess."

"You're a doll. I wouldn't want his Highness to get the wrong impression of single mothers—"

"I have the utmost respect for single parents, *chéri*."

The phone dropped out of Nola's hand, knocking Sheila's vase of roses over onto her appointment book.

"Yikes!" Sheila shouted.

"Hello? Hello? Nola?" Jill called from the receiver.

Del leaned near, lifted the receiver. Nola's heart stopped. "I believe Nola is finished."

In more ways than one, she thought.

Grinning, he said, "Sorry that I scared you, *chéri*."

"Me, too," she said, then moaned. How much had he heard? She eyed him closely, waiting for the bomb to drop. He remained grinning like a fool—oblivious to her conversation.

After Nola shoved Del out of the waiting room with the lie that having a single male around would make the pregnant mothers uncomfortable, she helped clean the mess, apologized profusely, and headed out into the hallway.

Del stood, leaning against the wall—talking to Olie!

Nola said another one of her made-up prayers and hurried over. "Hi, Dr. Goodman." Biting her lower lip she shoved her arm around Del's. With a tug, she said, "Tight schedule, doc. Make sure you check the notice for your department's inservice." Despite Del having a good seventy pounds on her, she yanked him down the hall.

Out of Dr. Goodman's earshot, Del planted his feet and asked, "What are you doing?"

She let him go. Good thing, cause that darn chemistry that made her skin sizzle was beginning to get to her. "Nothing. We have to go–"

"In my country we respect our physicians."

"I respect Olie...Dr. Goodman. He's a brilliant doctor. That's why he's my–" If she thought her skin sizzled from Del's touch, there was no comparison to the fire burning up her cheeks from that comment.

He touched her cheek. "No need to be embarrassed. Women in my country have their own doctors, too. Besides, *chéri*, I have known you...intimately."

Yeah, like that made her feel a heck of a lot better. She pushed his hand away, swallowed deeply and said, "Let's get back to work." With that she walked past him. He could stare at her back all he wanted because no way did she want him to see her face. It had to rival Henri's lovely cherry-red shade.

"Don't walk so fast, Nola," Del said, coming up behind.

"We have a lot to do." She pushed open the door to the stairs and paused. If Del hadn't found his way to the OB clinic she would have used the elevator. Looking at the metal staircase, it dawned on her that she'd have to climb seven flights of stairs. That couldn't be good for the baby.

"Something wrong?"

She swung around. "Nope. I just remembered there was something I wanted to show you on this floor." Peeking around him to make sure Olie had gone into the clinic, she let out a breath and said, "Come on," not having an inkling as to what she was going to show him.

Nola had worked here in the OR her entire career, which gave little reason to be at this end of the hospital. Now she had no idea what she was going to show Del. They passed the laundry, the reception desk for the west wing and now headed down a hall with brightly colored paintings on it. They appeared childlike so she thought maybe they'd moved the pediatric clinic down here.

"If I knew we'd be hiking so far today, I would have worn my Nike's," Del said.

"Good exercise." The end of the hallway loomed ahead. Oh great, a dead end. Now what?

Del looked forward and chucked. He placed his arm around her and pulled tight despite her trying to get away. "Are you trying to tell me something, *chéri?*"

Her shoulders tensed as she looked ahead.

"Your Children's Place," the sign said. The hospital employee's daycare center. She wiggled from his grasp. "What's that supposed to mean?" Please don't let him mention pregnancy.

He grinned wickedly. "Only that you brought me here to show me how wonderful it would be for us to make a—"

"Dream on, Your Highness." Her hand shook from his words. How did he manage to sound so sensual? "I brought you here to show you where the employee's children stay."

Del looked through the window at the kids jumping and running inside. "Why?"

"Why? Why?" Yeah, why? "Because it is interesting for someone who...right. I thought since you hadn't been to a grocery store or cleaners you might like to see a daycare center."

One eyebrow rose, he leaned near and said, "We have children in Mirabella."

She whacked his arm. "I know that. It's just that for parents who work, we have these places—"

"Mirabella is not some third world country, Nola. We, too, have daycare centers."

"Oh."

"Perhaps you thought we corralled all the youngins' into pens while their parents worked?" He did a darn good imitation of a hillbilly accent.

"Of course not. It's just—" She grabbed the handle. "Do you want to see it or not?" Please say no, she thought because right now she had no desire to look at adorable children with the father of her baby–when he had no clue that he was.

He placed his hand on top of hers. "As a matter of fact I'd like to see inside very much."

Nola stepped aside so he could pass. Then she turned toward the hallway and blew out a breath.

When she went to introduce herself to the woman in charge and tell her why they were here, the woman smiled first at Del, of course, then at Nola. "Good afternoon. May I help you?"

Nola hesitated. Hopefully this woman didn't have any friends in the OB clinic. Suddenly it occurred to her that her child would be coming here in a few months! "Well, we, that is he and I–"

"Yes? Oh wait, aren't you Holly Carmichael's friend?"

"No!"

Del looked at her. "I thought you two were best of friends."

Nola grinned. "Yes, we are. But...well, this is His Royal Highness Delmar Dupre." She leaned down to read the woman's nametag. "Mrs. Stephens. And, I...er...my job is to show him around the hospital. He wanted to see the daycare center."

The woman stood, holding her hand out to Del. Maybe she'd be mesmerized by the novelty of his behavior and forget Nola knew Holly.

He kissed her hand. She swooned. He said, "Charmed."

Nola grabbed onto the desktop. The baby chose that moment to tap-dance inside her. "Well, guess we can go upstairs now. Thanks–"

"Nola, I didn't see anything yet." He let Mrs. Stephen's hand go and said, "I really would like a short tour. If that is possible."

"Oh, yes," she purred.

Nola stood back as the woman came around the desk, pointed toward one of the helpers and said, "Mary, please show this nice man...I mean prince around."

While Mary walked over in a fog-induced state, make that a Del-induced state, Nola took a deep breath and let it out very slowly. The baby quieted down, but Mrs. Stephen's looked as if she'd need help getting back to her seat. She'd glued her focus on Del who was halfway across the room.

"You okay?" Nola asked.

"Um. He is gorgeous." She pulled herself together and walked to her seat. "I thought you'd come to do your paperwork for a slot–"

"No! I'll be back for that. No need to rush things." Before she could get Mrs. Stephen's confused look out of her vision, Nola hurried across the room. She had to get Del out of here fast. The hospital was closing in on her. Getting smaller and smaller as to where it was safe to go with His Royal Intruder.

His departure couldn't come too soon.

Almost tripping over a Tonka Truck, Nola grabbed onto a nearby shelf. Del turned.

"Are you all right?" he asked.

"Fine. All set?"

"Mary is going to show me where the little ones rest."

Nola hurried forward. "Hi, Mary. I'm Nola." She looked at Del. "A crib is a crib."

He shook his head and turned toward Mary. "I'm very interested. You see, we are building a large daycare center in one of my factories."

"Cool," purred Mary.

Nola collapsed into a chair that had to be only a foot high. Mickey Mouse glared at her from the nearby shelf. A toddler passed by, carrying Minnie. Nola swore the doll gave her a dirty look. She deserved it, too, after acting so weird. But she had a darn good reason. If Del ever found out....

Through the window of the nursery she watched Mary hand Del a little baby. Nola's mouth dried. He touched the child as if made of the finest crystal. Large hands cuddled the infant to his chest, and although she couldn't hear from here, she watched him mouth the words "Rock a Bye Baby."

Her heart fluttered.

"He's a natural. Isn't he?" Mrs. Stephens said from behind.

Nola shook her head. A teardrop trickled down her cheek. She'd broken her childhood vow of never crying again–looking at her baby's father, knowing he'd never hold *their* child–and, she'd broken her heart, too.

Chapter Ten

Over the next few days, Nola attended every one of Del's inservices. She told herself that she needed to be there, after all, she was put in charge as the "ambassador to Mirabella" as her boss had put it. Truth be told, she could have left after the first one. Del didn't need her help. The man was doing a fine job on his own–no great surprise.

Today, in the rear of the amphitheater, the second seat from the end, the one she chose all week, she straightened to watch him explain the latest laser surgery that could be accomplished with his country's equipment.

The technician dimmed the house lighting while Del pointed to the green beam of light on the projection screen. Even in the duskiness, she could see him. See every detail. Of course, some of her observations ran on memory. The twinkle in his eyes as he spoke proudly of the genius engineers in Mirabella that had developed this latest machine. The way his hands expressively conveyed what he had to say in his characteristic fluid strokes. And, she admitted, it was not too difficult to watch the way he moved easily across the stage, his voice never faltering, his hands never shaking.

Del was a confident man.

Loud applause snapped Nola's mind back to the amphitheater in time to hear Del say, "That concludes the question and answer session. If anyone has other questions, you may contact me here at this office." He pointed to the left of the stage.

She pulled herself up, readied to sneak out the back as soon as the crowd started to file out. No way did she want Del to know she was here–observing.

"Thank you. Before everyone leaves, however, I'd like to say a special thanks to the woman who helped me so much this first week."

Nola sunk down into her chair. Maybe he was talking about Ann?

"*Chéri?*" He looked directly at her.

"Oh God," she murmured. The entire roomful turned around in a collective stare. She smiled, nodded and looked to see Del's gaze on her–like a damn laser. She managed to wave and turned to look at her shoe as if that would take the focus off her. And, oh geez, he had to call her that stupid nickname! Now the entire hospital would rib her about it.

"Please come down. Ladies and Gentlemen, I'm certain you all know Ms. Nola St. Clair." She looked up in time to see him point at her. The crowd stared. Her heart flipped a good ten times, then she stood on legs of Jell-O.

Thank goodness there was a railing to hold onto as she made her way down the steps. When she reached the stage, he held out his hand. "I'll get you for this, Your Highness," she whispered, ignoring it.

"I look forward to that." Everyone in the room must have caught his mischievous leer. Nola's face burned hotter than a stupid laser.

She turned toward the doctors and nurses she'd worked with for years and plastered a smile on her face. "Well," she said into the microphone, "that concludes this inservice–"

"Yes, it does, *chéri*, however–" He bent and reached behind the podium–and pulled out a gigantic bouquet of yellow roses.

Nola wanted to run. Standing in front of nearly the entire hospital, feeling like a fool, she wanted to run–but not before she whacked him good with the darn roses.

He held them toward her, a grin on his face. Seemed as if the spotlight shone only on him, rays glistening on his golden skin, his teeth sparkling and midnight hair still dark despite the light. She sighed.

When she reached out, she caught a sniff of his cologne mixed with the fragrant roses, making her gaze drift to his eyes. Suddenly it seemed as if time slowed. She felt the roses in her hands before she realized she actually held them. She felt her heart beats pound against her chest. And, she felt like melting into a puddle when Del's gaze locked onto hers.

Midnight. The dark pools of midnight absorbed her. Took away her sound reasoning. Made her want to reach out and kiss him.

"I merely wanted to thank you publicly for all your help." He took her arm, most likely guessing the effect he had on her. And obviously knowing she couldn't move or speak. She couldn't even pull away. He looked out at the audience. "Thank you for coming. And remember, my technicians are on call twenty-four hours a day if you have any questions."

Nola heard a shuffling noise and blinked. The crowd, filing out of the amphitheater, blurred. Del's grasp tightened. Oh geez! She freed herself from his magical net and looked at him. "Um...thanks for the flowers. You didn't have to."

He smiled. Leaned near. Whispered, "I always do what I want."

She nearly lost it.

"I do appreciate your organizing everything so smoothly. The week has passed without a hutch."

"Hitch," she corrected.

He nodded. "Again I am grateful."

"Look, Del, I was only doing my job. Ann assigned you to me." She couldn't look at him as she spoke, or she knew she'd say things she didn't mean to. But right now, she needed to make it clear that their relationship was purely business–no matter how she felt, how she wanted it to be.

"I realize that, *chéri*. However, you did an exemplary job." He leaned near, brushed a kiss across her cheek and finished with, "I couldn't have done it without you. I'm certain the remainder of the inservices will run as smoothly."

He'd done it with that kiss. All she could manage was, "There are only two more left."

Del looked at Nola. "Only two more?" She nodded. He hoped he read the sadness in her eyes correctly. Convinced she didn't want him to leave, at least not alone, he took her hand into his. "Let's go away this weekend–"

She pulled free. "No. I can't do that. You know it." Her hand shook as she pushed a strand of hair from her forehead. "Stop asking me. Stop kissing me, and don't do things like buying me flowers again."

"You are not being honest, *chéri*." After this tiring week, he had little patience left.

By the looks of her, hackles raised, he at least got an emotional rise out of her. "Are you accusing me of lying?"

"Yes."

She shoved the roses at him. "Take these back."

Del pushed them toward her. "They are for your work, not your

125

heart."

She froze. He could hear her swallow deeply as if buying time. "I...I don't want them for whatever reason. And, I don't want you."

With that she turned and walked up the stairs of the amphitheater–roses still in hand. He smiled to himself.

"Stop lying to yourself, Nola. You can't deny the chemistry, the feelings between us."

She stopped on the last step and turned. Sucking in a deep breath she said, "Okay, Your Highness, I'll give you that one. Yeah, there is chemistry, but that doesn't mean a thing."

He started up the steps. She didn't move. Okay, that was good. "How can you say that?"

"Because, Del, lust doesn't make a relationship. Sure it's fun, but it's superficial. I feel chemistry with lots of good-looking–" Her hand flew to cover her lips.

He'd made it within reaching distance without her running out. "You wound me deeply."

"Shut up." She remained rooted on the spot.

"Let me take you somewhere so we can test your 'it's only chemistry' theory."

"I don't want to go away."

"You know, Nola. It's wonderful that you have so many friends here. That you are so well known throughout the hospital and have a nice place to live. But there is more to life than Soledad. I'm sorry for your past, but you really have become a hermit here."

She turned to go and made it to the door. He shoved his hand against it as she tried to open it. "This time you are staying to listen." He shoved his other hand against the door, trapping him between.

"Let me go!" She wiggled and tried to sneak beneath his outstretched arms.

He took her by the shoulders and held her despite her attempts to pull free. "I'm not hurting you and you are going to stay and listen. What future do you have here?"

Her muscles tensed beneath his touch. "I have a great life."

"Yes, at the moment. You work, have friends. But there is a world out there that you ignore. Why?"

She tried to push at his chest. He tightened his hold. "I don't have to answer any of this. Let me go."

"Not until you *do* answer." He leaned near, looked into her eyes. He'd almost expected to see fear, but thank goodness his action had not frightened her. She must have known he wouldn't hurt her because, despite her denial, she knew how he felt–how she felt about him. That he was sure of. "If you want me to let go, tell me why you don't ever leave this town."

"I don't have any reason to." Her bottom lip jetted forward. He wanted to kiss her, but knew if he softened, she'd note his weakening and escape.

"There is a wonderful world out there. So much to see, to experience. Are you really going to be happy here, maybe never having a family? Perhaps for the rest of your life?"

Fear widened her eyes. He released his hold a bit. The intention was not to scare her, but to get her to admit...yet the mention of family frightened her.

"My having a family or not is none of your concern."

"It is when I want to make that family with you, be the father of your children–"

Where she got the strength from, he'd never know, but she managed to shove him so hard, he fell into one of the seats. She stood staring at him.

"It seems you have let your mother's actions effect you, *chéri*. You won't even entertain the idea of having a family because of her. You fear abandonment so you won't let a man into your life. Hiding away in this tiny town, you feel secure. Is that it?" He pushed himself up and stood.

"My mother has nothing to do with this. I don't want to go away with you because...I don't have feelings for you."

"That is a lie."

She glared at him. Her lips curled. "No, it isn't."

She'd managed to raise his hackles now. "Prove it."

"I don't have to prove anything to you."

He leaned near. "Then prove it to yourself." That one had her speechless. Good. "Like I said. Prove it to yourself, because when I kissed you–you kissed back. And I *know* when a woman wants me." He turned to walk back to the office. She grabbed his arm.

"You arrogant son of–"

He turned, looked at her and laughed. "Maybe. But at least I'm an honest son of a–"

"Okay. I'll prove it to you once and for all. Under one condition."

He leaned against the chairs, folded his arms, and held his chin in his hand. "I'm not used to having to accept conditions."

"Of course not. You are used to getting whatever you want. But I'm not about to give you whatever you want nor am I used to having someone call me a liar. I intend to prove to you that I am not. I want you to agree that once this weekend is over, and you learn the truth, you will leave the United States and never contact me...again."

"Agreed."

"I'll make the arrangements as to where we go. Separate rooms. Separate beds."

"Agreed."

"You will drive your own car to the town of Cloudbluff. It's on the map. Anyone in town can give you directions to the Inn of the Heavens. It's the highest peek of the mountains surrounding Soledad. I'll be there at seven tonight." She sucked in a breath. "And as soon as you see how wrong you are and that I'm not lying–you leave and come back alone. Then...you go back to Mirabella."

"Agreed." He started down the stairs and looked back. "Be prepared, Magnolia, to admit the *truth*."

Nola watched him walk down the stairs and wanted to throw the beautiful roses at him. What nerve! He'd pulled out all the stops with that one. Was Del right? Was she setting her baby up for a life secluded in Soledad? Deep inside she knew she was–but her life here was wonderful. It could be the same for her child.

That was right and she'd prove it to him. She'd go out of town with him on this stupid weekend because of the baby, then she could get rid of him forever. Her life could return to normal until the baby was born. Her baby. She'd felt so good lately, she nearly forgot she was pregnant until the baby kicked. Rubbing her hand across her abdomen, she smiled.

She reached up to push a hair from her eyes and inhaled Del. Her legs weakened. Urges flooded her inside. Sensual urges that said she wanted him. It *had been* a lie about chemistry with other men because no one had ever made her feel like this–like she wanted to make love to him against her logical thinking, her sensible wishes.

Maybe agreeing *was* a mistake.

Would she have the courage to drive out of town and the strength to resist Del?

Of course she would, because of the baby.

She went to open the door to the hallway then remembered she needed to get her papers from Del's office before leaving for the weekend. Oh great. Maybe she could come back later. Looking at her watch, she knew there wasn't time. She had to give them to Ann before she missed her today. On Fridays no one hung around.

"He doesn't scare me," she muttered, turned and walked down the stairs. At the bottom, she sucked in a breath, straightened her shoulders until they ached and walked toward Del's temporary office.

She knocked. Expecting him to say "come in," she jumped back when the door opened. He stood with his jacket off, shirtsleeves rolled above firmly muscled arms.

The question of her having the strength to resist him was going downhill fast.

She pushed past him. "I need my papers for Ann."

Thank goodness he stayed near the door. "No problem. Actually, I have to run up to the OR, too. Care to share an elevator?" He grabbed his navy blazer from a nearby chair and flipped it over his shoulder. Then, he grinned at her.

"Very funny. You go ahead. I'll get what I need."

"I don't mind waiting–"

"I mind it. Go or the weekend is off."

"I'll see you in Cloudbluff."

She groaned. "Yeah." Soon after the door shut, she rifled through the stack of papers to get out of here quickly. Del's damned scent choked the air out of the room. She couldn't think clearly if she smelled the spicy fragrance amid the clicks and whirs of the machinery. "Oh, wait!" She jumped up to catch him. "Do you want me to turn off the power–" She looked up to see the amphitheater door closing. Darn, she'd missed him. Well, he'd taken his jacket, so she figured he wasn't coming back.

She shoved the papers into a pile and reached to shut off the master power switch. Her eyes focused on the monitor. Without a thought, she shoved the zero. "Oh, geez, what did I do?" As the monitor crackled, she went to shut it off, but figured she better wait. If it was like a computer, it needed to do its thing full cycle before the power could be turned off. Not wanting to harm any of Del's equipment–technical equipment that is–she waited.

"Who is there?" a male voice asked.

Nola's leaned back and stared at the monitor. Oh no! King Leon blinked a few times as he came into focus.

"My. My." He chuckled. "How interesting to see a beautiful woman materialize before my eyes."

She'd forgotten how jovial the white headed man could be. "Hello, Your Royal Highness."

He cleared his throat. "Hello, *Mademoiselle*. You are well?"

She smiled. "Yes, sir. And you are looking quite well, too."

His complexion grew ruddy. "How nice of you to say. The queen is always bothering me about eating healthy, exercising." He groaned. "Fruits and grains. Who needs roughage at my age?"

Nola laughed. "I'm sure she means well. A man in your position needs to stay fit."

"My boys see to that."

She rolled her eyes at the thought of Del. "I'll bet they do."

"Damien, the rascal, won't sit still for two seconds."

She raised an eyebrow. Rascal isn't the term she'd use for him.

Before she could say goodbye, he continued, "Now Delmar, the quieter one, he is a son you could trust to leave for hours. The boy will remain wherever, busying himself."

King Leon laughed so heartily, Nola felt a tug at her heart. Del would never be able to talk of his child like this. But it was odd that the king spoke of his sons as if they were–

"You know, young lady, they are twins."

"Yes, Your Highness, I knew that."

"Looked exact at birth, that's where the problem came in. Now they've grown into their own selves."

She really didn't want to be discussing Del or his childhood with his father. Standing, she said, "Well, it was a pleasure to see you again–"

"Have we met before?"

Nola sank down into the chair. Did Del have that many women in his life these past months that the king didn't even remember her? She'd spent weeks in the palace for crying out loud. Well, what did it matter. "Yes, Your Highness. I'd met you months ago when Del brought me to the palace. I'm Nola St. Clair. From America."

He leaned into the monitor. She nearly laughed as his nose seemed huge the closer he got. "Are you one of his nannies?"

Nola froze. Nannies? The king thought she was one...he spoke of "the boys" as if he believed they really were boys. Little boys. Not men. This was odd. She was worried about him now, but didn't know what to do. "Your Highness, is Henri there?"

"Oh no. That old busybody. A regular snoop. I sneaked away from him after lunch." He chuckled.

The hairs on the back of Nola's neck rose. "Perhaps you should find him?"

"The man is a pest."

Nola smiled. "All right. What about the queen?"

"The woman is a pest."

Wow. She was surprised to hear him say that. "Perhaps–" She hated to even mention the name, but if it would help the king from coming to any harm, she would force herself. "–Damien. Is he around there?"

The king's brows furrowed. "That boy is–"

"Right behind you, Father."

Nola gripped the arms of the chair. The tone of his voice still made her skin prickle. Mirabellan engineers were geniuses to make a monitor with such exact sound quality that Damien's voice could cause such a reaction in her.

She could see his hand on the king's shoulder, the Dupre family ring on his finger. "I'll take care of things, father. Go wait in the library."

Nola's hand shook as she reached for the power switch. The heck with worrying about the equipment. Before she could touch the button, he said, "Ah, *Mademoiselle* St. Clair. How odd to find you conversing with the king. What did you have to discuss with him?"

"That's none of your business, Damien."

"Prince Damien."

She rolled her eyes. "You can shut that thing off at your end now because that is what I am going to do here." Her finger touched the button.

"Tell your lover that Princess Angelica and I have news."

She froze. Maybe there was something important she'd need to tell Del. "He's not my lover."

"Smart woman. However, as much as that news would thrill me–you are a liar." He leaned back, his arms behind his head. Damien was quite handsome, much like Del as his father had said. They were exact twins, but he wore his hair much longer, unruly. The eyes could never compare. Where Del's were deep as the night, Damien's were a shade the likes of which she'd never seen. Yellow, reminding her of a movie prop some actor would wear in a horror film. Definitely a shade of repulsion.

"Well, it was nice talking to you–"

"No it wasn't, Nola. You don't like me–"

"As well I shouldn't."

Even across thousands of miles, his eerie laughter ran chills up her spine. "Hey, I call it like I see it. Not like my brown-nosed brother."

She shut her eyes, willing her memory not to relive the day he told her if she married Del she'd ruin his chance at being king. "I'm sure you do. Goodbye, Prince."

He laughed, leaned near the monitor. "Tell my brother the good news I found out minutes ago–I'm going to be a father."

Nola gasped. She could barely breath and it was impossible to swallow. Damien and Princess Angelica were expecting, too!

"Aw, you look so disappointed. Too bad you didn't beat us to the punch–"

The picture flickered. Nola leaned near, ready to turn off the monitor, get him out of her mind. Before she could press the button, Henri appeared. She heard muffled voices as if one had his hand over the microphone.

Damien stood. Leaning near, she saw Henri, face wrinkled in

anger, talking to the prince. Suddenly the prince walked out of the picture–but not before he turned and glared at Nola. She shuddered even though he wasn't in the room.

"Good day, *Mademoiselle*."

Nola leaned back, her body shaken. "Hi, Hank."

"I am sorry if–"

"I'm fine. Oh, Henri, King Leon was on before. Is he all right?"

Henri hesitated. He'd always been a pillar of decorum. He'd have made a great Englishman. "The king is fine. I shall need to go now–"

She sat forward. "Henri, one thing."

"*Oui?*"

"Damien...said to tell Del something. But I don't think it's my place–"

"He often fabricates thing. Perhaps he is trying to start trouble with some lie?"

"That could be, but it seems farfetched that he would say that Princess Angelica and he are expecting–"

Henri's eyes widened. He raised a shaky hand to run across his brow. He didn't know! Oh geez, she was getting in way too deep here. "Expecting?"

"A baby. He wanted me to tell Del, but that's none of my business– Are you all right?" He looked ill as if he were to have a stroke. "Henri? You are scaring me. You believe it's true?"

"Unfortunately I do."

"You don't look well." She touched the monitor.

"I am all right, Nola."

He'd never called her by her name. Something was wrong. "You don't seem too happy. Geez, I was thrilled when I found out I was preg–"

In a flash of colors, Henri leaned so near his face distorted. "*Mademoiselle?*"

She couldn't breath. Every attempt to swallow was stopped by the fact that her mouth was drier than the wooden desk. Waving her hand, she readied to turn off the screen.

"Don't!"

She hesitated.

His voice softened in a fatherly tone. "Please, do not turn it off."

"I..." She sighed. It was way too hard to lie to Henri.

"You are–"

She nodded. "Henri, I must ask that you not breathe a word of this...I mean it is–" Not Del's baby she wanted to lie. But couldn't. Maybe it was Henri's honest face staring at her. Maybe it was the fact that fear had her mind paralyzed, and she couldn't even finish her sentence. Or maybe, she admitted, it was that she knew if Del found out the truth someday she'd experience true fear the likes of which she'd never known.

"Prince Delmar does not know?"

She shook her head. "Please don't say anything."

"I respect your wishes, *Mademoiselle*, I think you know that. However–" Now he seemed nervous. There was something very important he wanted to say, yet hesitated. For several seconds, he remained frozen on the screen.

Her heart thudded loudly. Sweat broke out on her palms as Henri paused his words.

As she leaned near, waiting–she wondered if she wanted to hear.

Chapter Eleven

Nola knew she couldn't get out of Del's office if she wanted to. Fear had her rooted to the spot. She'd told him about the baby! Now Henri's words had her momentarily speechless. Feeling like this, she was certain she didn't want to hear what followed his "however."

This was the second worse day of her life.

"Are you all right, *Mademoiselle*?" A warm concern filled Henri's eyes.

She nodded. Holding onto both arms of the chair, she wished she'd never pressed the damn zero and brought Mirabella into her life full force. It was bad enough having Del following her around all day, now this. Possibly, she'd ruined her life. How she regretted ever leaving Soledad. "I'll be all right. I just want to go home."

"You are not physically ill?"

"No." Only emotionally, she thought as her heart ached. "I'll be fine." If she got up and left, ignoring the fact that Henri had more to say, she could get the weekend with Del over with. She'd prove to him that he was wrong–if she were a good enough actress, and he'd have to fulfill his agreement to leave.

She looked at Henri.

Shutting her eyes, she asked, "What were you going to say?"

"Again, I will never tell His Highness about your baby. However, you need to know something."

Her eyes widened. Was there some disease they passed on to their children? Maybe some mutant genes in the Dupre family? She thought of Damien and shuddered. "Yes?" Her voice came out so weakly, Henri hadn't heard. She leaned toward the built-in microphone and asked, "What do I need to know?"

"When the princes were born, their mother had been on her way to the summer residence. A storm washed out the road, and she detoured through the village of Saint Pierre. The king had gone ahead days before, myself at his side, so the queen was only with her servants. When they had to stop for the night, a villager took them in. The queen went into labor–" He paused, wiped a handkerchief across his brow. "A midwife delivered the boys during the storm."

"Wow. Good thing everything turned out so well." She hesitated. Did she really want to hear more. "Was...there a problem with the babies?"

Henri sighed. "In the confusion, the woman inadvertently mixed up the time of birth for each twin. Thankfully she was trained in delivery, yet living in the mountainous area, she had little need for clocks with batteries. When the power had gone out, the delivery took place by candlelight. She could never swear which boy was born first."

Nola wrinkled her forehead. This was interesting but she didn't see the point. At least he hadn't mentioned any problems with their health. "I don't understand what difference—"

"I apologize for my oversight. Coming from America you have no need to concern yourself with primogeniture."

"No...actually, Hank, I don't know what the word means."

He chuckled. At least that helped ease some of the tension that had her neck near to spasm. "Heritage. Order of succession. The firstborn becomes king."

"Oh my." She fidgeted in her seat, wishing she could skip the history lesson and go home. Although she'd accidentally told Henri about the baby, she knew she could trust him. That made her feel much better. "That does seem like a dilemma."

"*Oui*. Soon after the birth of the twins, the National Council, who is under the king's rule in our land and there to guide him, put pressure on His Royal Highness. They wanted him to establish a rule of succession to solve the problem."

"What a decision for a father to have to make."

"*Oui*. It was not easy. King Leon suffered over the choices for weeks. He knew he needed to make it clear, but how to chose between two babies. So, he ruled that the first of the princes to marry would succeed—"

"Oh my God! That means Damien is in line first—"

"King Leon knew a rivalry would ensue if the rule were not more specific. He feared his sons marrying for the wrong reason."

"Guess he knew Damien pretty well even as a newborn."

Henri nodded. "He was a very active baby. No one could hold him for long." He wiped at his brow. "Being a gifted ruler, the king said the princes not only had to be married, but the first to—produce an heir would be first in line—"

She knew Henri kept speaking, but she couldn't hear. The baby she carried, months further along than Damien's, was Del's means to be king someday–and the hope for the future of Mirabella.

"I have to go now, Henri."

The static drowned out his final "*Oui*."

The drive home was the longest trip Nola had ever taken. The baby chose this time to wake, thumping her inside so she couldn't forget she had a decision to make.

A decision that would affect her and her baby's lives.

The sun rested on the crest of the western mountain range, reminding her of her plans with Del. She couldn't go to him now, not feeling this confused. All he'd have to do was capture her in his web, and she wouldn't be in control of her actions–her words.

Brilliant golds, reds, and flames of orange peeked from the rocky tops. She loved New Mexico. She loved Soledad's quaintness. Its proximity to the canyons and desert surrounding the eastern side, wrapping around to the south while the mountain range flanked the north and west gave her everything she needed in scenery–seclusion.

It was as if her town was isolated from the rest of the world.

She pulled over to the side of the road near a giant Saguaro. With tears streaming down her face, she looked at the quiet stretch of road. Sand crept onto the pavement as if the desert tried to claim back what belonged to it before man had intruded. No one was allowed to put billboard signs in this area between the hospital and her apartment complex. The ordinance kept the area natural. That's why she drove this way each day. She loved the seclusion, the arid scenery–and it was home.

Angry with herself for crying, she decided that maybe she had no choice. Facing the truth hurt. Although she'd always believed that crying made her vulnerable to more pain, maybe it was more a relief to let it out. The vow she'd made to herself as a child came from thinking tears were a sign of weakness–and they gave satisfaction to the fact that her mother had abandoned her. She'd never wanted to all out admit it, although it was made painfully clear when her mother brought her to the Social Service office that final day.

That was the last time she'd cried–until now.

She walked near the giant cactus. Shadows flowed beneath her feet as the last of the sun's rays burned into the Saguaro. Looking at her watch, she gasped. Six fifteen. She'd never make it home to pack and get to Cloudbluff in time. Holly had been there several times, even tried to entice Nola to go with stacks of brochures, so she knew how long the trip would take. She wasn't certain of the directions although Holly had insisted it was easy to find on the map.

Del would be waiting for her.

But could she go and not tell him about the baby?

Del opened the door to Room Forty-seven of the Inn of the Heavens. It felt as if he'd stepped back in time. The room was beautiful in a rustic sort of way. Wooden beams crossed the ceiling while darkened knots in the floor told a hint of their age. He felt like some cowboy he'd seen in the old Clint Eastwood movies he loved so much. Even in his country the actor was a giant star.

He walked in, shut the door and placed his suitcase on the brown leather couch. His step quickened as he looked at the clock in the center of the onyx horse above the mantel. Nola would be here any minute. He'd actually expected to run into her in the lobby, but the clerk informed him she had not checked in as yet.

Good. Now he had time to prepare. Opening his suitcase, he lifted out a bottle of champagne and a bottle of Pinch his favorite Scotch. The champagne was to share. The scotch, well, that he always craved after.... He chuckled. It was his one vice after making love. The last time he'd drank the Pinch was.... Visions of himself and Nola had his heart beating harder as the memories came more vivid. He set both bottles on the counter.

Reaching into his suitcase, he took out two crystal goblets he'd carefully wrapped in towels and set them on the coffee table. In a small pouch on the side, he felt around and pulled out a jar of caviar and a roll of crackers.

Inside the wet bar freezer he found trays of ice which he poured into the bathroom sink then set the champagne in to chill. Hopefully it would chill fast. She'd be here any second. Carefully he set his watch on the table, facing away from the bed. He hurried to remove his suitcase into the closet.

On the way, he straightened two pillows, opened the drapes near the bed to reveal mountains flocked with slender Aspens. Thank goodness no one would pass this way since the room overlooked a cliff. Privacy was important. Having the fabulous view didn't hurt. He'd take all the help he could get.

Opening the door, he shoved the suitcase into the closet, closed the door and looked at his watch. She had to have checked in by now. Feeling like a giddy teen, he sat on the edge of the bed, lifted the phone receiver and dialed the front desk. "Please connect me to Ms. St. Clair's room."

"One moment, sir," the clerk said.

He hoped the fifty he'd slipped the clerk had Nola unpacking in the room directly next to his.

The line clicked. "*Chéri?*"

"Um, its still me, sir," the clerk said. Del felt his forehead wrinkle. He slumped back onto the bed, shoving off his shoes before resting his feet on the spread.

"Can't you connect me to Ms. St. Clair?"

"I'm afraid not."

"Then give me her room number, and I shall knock on her door."

The clerk hesitated. Del felt another small bribe might be in order. "Even if I was allowed to give out guest's room numbers, she isn't here."

Del sat upright. He looked at his watch. Seven forty-five. "Call me the second she checks in."

He hung up. The first thing he thought about was that she might have had car trouble. Hopefully she carried a cell phone. Since he'd never ridden in her car, he could only wish she did. Of course, it would be like Nola not to. She more than likely knew how to repair her own car if need be and didn't think she'd ever need the expertise of an automotive mechanic.

Del kept looking at his watch. The time sped far too quickly. After two more phone calls to make certain that the clerk hadn't forgotten to tell him when Nola arrived, he got up and shoved on his shoes. Grabbing his car keys, wallet and hotel key, he headed out the door.

When he opened it, he froze. Nola stood there staring at him, yet looking past him. She knew she looked crazy, but she felt just that way. Del grabbed her arm so hard it hurt, but she'd only seen concern in his eyes, so she didn't pull back.

"I'm all right. Can I come in?"

"Where were you?" He stepped aside, shoved the door shut with his foot. "Your luggage?"

"I didn't bring any. Look, Del, I–" She eased free of his hold and walked to the window. "The view must be lovely."

"If you came before sunset you would have seen it."

She swung around. "I didn't want to come."

He shook his head. "You promised–"

"I know what I said, but I never even went home from the hospital. I stayed by some stupid Saguaro cactus for what had to be hours. If it wasn't for a flashlight Holly had given me for Christmas to keep in my trunk, I would never have been able to read the map to get here. I...it was very difficult to drive here. I had what amounted to several panic attacks after leaving Soledad."

He looked scared, concerned. "Are you–"

"I said I'm fine. But I almost didn't come."

Del sucked in a deep breath. He felt as if he were going to explode when he said, "If this is all so difficult for you, maybe you were correct today."

Nola's heart jolted. "No!"

He walked into the bathroom and grabbed the bottle from the sink. "The ice melted," he said as the cork popped, sending a spray of champagne into the air.

"I'm sorry I'm so late, but...I am here."

Del grabbed a plastic glass from the counter, tore off the wrapper and poured the sparkling liquid. He took a long sip, set the glass down. "You want some?"

"No. Thanks."

He shook his head, walked to the couch and sat down. She looked at the coffee table. Two goblets. Caviar. Her heart tightened as she noticed the bottle of Pinch. She knew very well when he craved the scotch. Del continued to drink in silence.

Nola sucked in a breath and walked toward him. She'd like to keep going, out the door, but she couldn't. Instead, she had to do what she came her for.

She owed it to Del.

"I thought something happened to you," he said, taking a long sip of champagne.

"I'm sorry if I worried you." She forced her feet to move until she neared the couch. Anger wrinkled his forehead and the depths of his eyes deepened. Her hands shook as she seated herself next to him.

"I wanted this to all be so special."

She nodded, looked at the table. "I see that."

He sat forward, set his drink down with such force that spills dotted the tabletop. "What you don't see, Nola, is the truth. You have clouded your judgement with your fears that you can't see, can't admit how you really feel."

"That's not true. You are making a difficult situation so much harder." She leaned back and sighed.

"I'm sorry, *chéri*, if being here is so difficult for you. I had no intention of forcing you into something you didn't want." He pushed up to stand. "Obviously I *was* wrong this afternoon. If it pains you so much to be with me, then I shall leave."

She grabbed his arm. "No."

"Stop it, Nola. Stop tugging my heart back and forth."

She stood, not letting him go. "I...don't want you to go." She ran her hand along his arm, felt the stiffened muscles. His eyes remained cool. Her fingers shook.

"I am so very tired of all this."

"I'm sorry. Really, Del. I came here because...."

Del looked into her eyes. His anger had clouded his vision, and he hadn't noticed the pain before. "Because why?"

She looked upward, touched at his face. Without a word, she stood on her tiptoes and kissed him. "Please don't ask me right now."

He hesitated. This was all too confusing, and he was a man trained to keep a clear head. She was hurting, he had no doubt. But why? Why was she so late? Why did she say it was so difficult to come here other than the actual driving?

And why was he not interested in any of those answers right now?

He grabbed her with such force, she stumbled. One goblet crashed to the wooden floor as he grasped her head with both hands. His lips took her with a furry he had never known. Anger had led his actions earlier, but now, desire won out.

He had to have Nola, or he wouldn't be responsible for his actions. Pressure built inside his head, thundering against his temples so that he knew she could feel the vibrations as her skin touched his. "I do not want to hurt you, but–"

"You're not." She ran her hands behind his head, fingers pressing into his hair, sending signals that would relieve his hunger. A hunger he had felt far too long.

"I cannot stop," he said in words that came out a whisper.

Her fingers stilled. Del's vision blurred red. If she had come here to taunt him, then claim she was right, he feared his reaction. Right now he could not think straight. She pushed at his chest.

"Stay there."

He took a deep breath, blew it out in a loud force. "Don't do this, Nola. Don't play with–"

Purposefully, she touched at the top button of her blouse. She'd taken to wearing such loose fitting clothing, it made him all the more aroused to picture what lay beneath. Inching her fingers down, she undid each button, until the purple silk slid to reveal the lace of her white bra.

"I...if you go any further–"

Wicked. That's the term he'd use for her smile. "Shut up, Your Highness," she said in a throaty voice that stirred him inside.

Del collapsed onto the couch. He'd always been a strong man, worked out religiously, but right now, watching her peel the material from her shoulder, he could no longer stand.

Damn.

His gaze followed the flowing material as it pooled around her feet. Sometime earlier she'd slipped off her shoes and stood in black nylons. Obviously he'd been too angry to notice, but now even the sight of her stocking feet made him lustful. He wanted to swallow. Hoped it would ease the dryness in his mouth, but no luck. Nothing could get a cell of his body to move. If he died right now, watching his Nola, he'd be content.

No, he didn't want to miss a thing.

Nola hesitated when her fingers came to the button of her skirt. Twice she'd run into the ladies' room off the lobby before coming up here. When she was certain no one was there, she'd stood in the mirror, moving in all different angles to see if she showed. Thankfully, a slight bulge and fuller hips was all she detected. However, the way Del's gaze had locked onto her chest, he'd noticed the fullness of her breasts and wouldn't mention the slight bulge.

Well, there was no stopping now.

If she tried to leave, she wouldn't blame him if he tackled her. Besides, no way in hell did she want to go anywhere.

She'd finally admitted one truth.

"*Chéri*? You cannot make me wait—"

She laughed. The throaty, sultry sound had Del moan. If she'd practiced it, she would never have been able to laugh so sensually. "Sorry." With that, she snapped the button through its hole, ran the zipper down, and stepped out of the skirt when it hit the floor. Leaning a bit closer, she looked into his eyes. Lust. Wanting. Good. No suspicion as to why she'd put on a few pounds.

Del started to stand, only to feel her hand push down on his shoulder.

"Un huh."

He leaned back, running his fingers through his hair. She lifted her chin, gave a sultry smile, and unhooked one nylon from the lacy white corset-like outfit she wore. He had no idea what the thing was called, but, running his tongue across his lips, it didn't make a damn bit of difference.

Her foot lifted and rested on his knee. "Oh God," he murmured while she rolled the nylon down, off the tip of her toes and sailed it across the room. He waited until she did it with the other, but when the snap popped on that one, she took his hand, guided it to the top so very close...oh Jesus...he might not be able to control himself much longer. Cursing his shaking fingers, he pulled the nylon down and off. Blowing out a huge breath, he heard Nola laugh. This time it was more a giggle than the sexy laugh she'd managed before. It wasn't an annoying sound such as a teenager would make—more a deeper tone that had his libido doing backflips.

She took his plastic glass, handed it to him. He nodded as the liquid momentarily relieved his dryness. He didn't trust himself to say "thanks."

Above his glass he watched her reach across him to flip off the light. Rays from the bathroom gave a dusky glow to the room. Who'd have thought the amount of light could make a sensual experience more so?

As she pulled back, her breast brushed across his cheek. He fiddled in his seat, ran his fingers through his hair.

She chuckled, deeply. "You've messed it." With a whisk of her hand, she ran her fingers across his head. He could care less what he looked like, because soon his head would burst into flames anyway. What did it matter if burning hair looked unruly?

"Stand," she commanded.

He took the hand she offered. If he didn't, he'd still be sitting. She reached up, kissed him deeply and ran her naughty fingers down his chest, ripping buttons off in their wake. He moaned when her touch found its way beneath the fabric. "*Cheri.*"

"*Oui.*" The whispered word nearly had him embarrassing himself in a premature act. She guided his head down to make him watch as she unsnapped his jeans, ran the zipper down, and eased the fabric off his hips. He grabbed the pants, throwing them across the room. Good thing the light was not on or his body would not be the only thing on fire tonight.

Nola pressed against him, kissing him.

He opened his mouth, felt her tongue enter—and the rest was the damnedest, most glorious blur.

Chapter Twelve

Del leaned back to look at Nola sleeping in his arms and took a sip of his Pinch scotch. The liquid warmed his throat, but he'd never felt heat as he had the past few...he looked at the clock...hours.

The time was well spent, he thought, grinning.

He pulled her closer, careful not to wake her. She stirred, smiled, and gave a gentle snore. He had to control his laugh, lest he wake her. After he took the final sip of scotch, he set the glass on the bedside table, smiled at the tiny cacti on her nails and shut his eyes.

No doubt he'd have fabulous dreams tonight.

"Del?"

He opened his eyes, wiped the strands of hair from her eyes. "I thought you were asleep."

"I guess I dozed, but, we need to–"

He touched a finger to his lip. "That's only in movies that a man can perform over and over, *chéri*, much as I'd like to."

Her laughter tickled his chest. She pulled herself up, darkened nipples peeking from beneath the sheets. She'd grown much fuller than he'd remembered from in his dreams. Running a finger across the darkness, he leaned over and kissed one tip. "Perhaps–" He kissed the other. "–I'll give it the old college try."

She slapped at his shoulder. "I'm trying to be serious."

He didn't like the look in her eyes. Not that he was a man who feared much, no, actually he'd often surprised himself with his daring. He wasn't reckless as Damien, but there wasn't much Del feared in life.

Except being ignored.

She gave him a pleading look. "Actually, I can't talk like this." Shoving off the sheets, she stood and collected her clothes from the floor.

Del jumped up. "What's wrong?"

She pushed him back onto the bed. "I need a few minutes."

He watched her walk across the room, having the damnedest time holding back as he eyed her nakedness.

Once in the bathroom, Nola shoved on the shower and stepped into the warmth. Oh, her body could more than likely use a cold shower to cool the heat Del had produced in her–what a knack he had. But she didn't want to shock her system and hurt the baby. Laughing, she rubbed shampoo into her hand. Life couldn't get any better, she thought. She'd just made spectacular love to Del, she was pregnant.... The door creaked open. "What are you–"

Water pooled on the floor as Del opened the shower door and stepped in. "You said you wanted to–" He leaned down and kissed her.

"Talk," she murmured. Earlier, their lovemaking had started with such force, her mind hadn't been able to comprehend, to think. Sure the pleasure Del had given her was right up there with rockets, fireworks, and shooting stars. Now that her thoughts had time to regroup, she needed to be serious.

He ran a soapy finger along her neck, between the cleft of her breasts. The water could have been zero degrees and she would have felt as if her blood boiled. She moaned as he touched the tip of one breast–and decided serious could wait.

"So, talk." He kissed her, leaned against the shower stall and stared at her.

"Later," she said against his cheek. Water pelted their bodies as he pulled her close. Wet skin could still generate a hell of lot of electricity.

He held her outward, smiling at her as if they stood in the rain. "You look as adorable as a wet puppy."

"Yeah, right." She curled her lip. "I'm sure with this hairdo I do." Pushing strands of wet hair back, she laughed. "How do you manage to look so damn good even wet? It's not fair."

He gave a leer. "Lucky, I guess."

Nola would have loved to continue, but she had to tell Del what she knew. She pushed him toward the shower door. "Get out and let me finish."

He stood firm. "Nope. I kinda like it in here, *cheri*." With that he grinned, looking down at her body. She had the urge to grab a towel despite the water splashing them.

"Come on. It'll get cold in here. Let me get out and get dressed. Then we'll talk."

"We can talk fine in here." He twisted the shower nozzle to a fine mist, and pushed the handle to warm the water. "Better?"

"Yes, but, I really want to get out."

"Anything that you say, you can say to me now. Our nakedness lends itself to the truth."

If only he knew how true that was, she thought, feeling as if her abdomen had just enlarged. Del took her into his hold. "Talk."

There was something special about the two of them secluded in the shower. It gave her the feeling as if she and Del were the only two in the world–at least the only two who mattered. He'd been right, and she was glad since it made what she had to tell him much easier.

And, she certainly had his undivided attention.

"Okay." She hesitated. "You're sure you don't want to get out?"

He leaned near. Water glistened on his golden skin, droplets clung to his eyelashes giving him a magical look. He'd done his magic on her for sure. "*Oui.*"

Finally she had the courage to tell him.

Not that it was easy, though. She still had concerns for her baby, but they'd lessened considerably after she and Del had made love. He had a right to know. And, she told herself, she had to tell him for Mirabella. She'd never felt loyalty to anyone before. A mother who didn't love her had destroyed her very foundation. Now was her chance to help an entire country–to exercise some kind of loyalty.

"Del, I'm...pregnant with your child."

Her skin numbed to the feel of the water spray. As if a weight had been lifted off her shoulders, she stood straighter, her heart lifted, a joy she'd never known filled her. The ecstasy of being pregnant heightened, as she would never have expected. What a relief to have the truth out!

Nothing could ruin this moment.

Then, she looked at Del.

His features froze beneath the droplets of hot water. Maybe the news was sinking in gradually. After all, she told herself, this news had to come out of left field. "Del? Are you all–"

"Let me get this straight. You are going to have my child?" He gripped the faucet.

"Um, hmm. Exciting, isn't it?"

"It certainly is, Nola. You've known this for sometime?" He

moved away.

She figured he needed to get out of the spray to think about the wonderful news. "Months." She reached out to him.

He pulled away. "That is why you were going to marry Rusty."

It wasn't a question. Suddenly the water cooled. Nola's heart beat a bit faster. "Yes." She pushed the nozzle toward hot, but the temperature in the shower stall remained cold.

Del turned to her. She'd never seen that look in his eyes before, or in anyone's. The patter of the water stilled, her world slowed. He became her immediate focus. "Don't you see, Del, my baby needed a father."

"It *has* a father."

"Yes, but I couldn't tell you. I didn't want you to marry me because–"

"Why now, Nola?"

The way he said her name was disconcerting. She thought she hated being called "*chéri*," but he'd always said it with such passion, such emotion. Now when he spoke her name his tone was flat, cold.

"I...when I was in your office, Damien came on the monitor." She wrapped her arms around her shoulders, telling herself it was to keep warm when she knew it was to hide her nakedness, her vulnerability.

He gave an impatient sigh. "So?"

"He said to tell you...Princess Angelica is pregnant."

At least now Del's eyes showed some emotion, only she'd rather not see such hatred, the anger.

"Henri interrupted. I accidentally slipped and told him about...our baby. He told me about the rule of succession."

How could she get such a strong feeling of him ignoring her is such an intimate setting? But she did. When she reached to touch him, he pulled back. "Don't you see, Del, I did it for your country. I'd been wrong before, trying to marry Rusty. I admit that now, damn it."

"That is one thing you are correct about."

Her patience was draining out much like the shower water running down the drain. "I didn't have to tell you now, you know?"

He looked directly at her. "You told me to help my country. Not because I have a *right* to know."

"Yes. No–"

She'd have expected the shower door to shatter into a million pieces with the force he'd shoved against it. Not being able to move, all she could do was watch. He didn't even grab a towel as he walked out of the room. In the mirror she watched him grab his jeans, shove them on with such vigor, she flinched. With his shirt and shoes in his hand, he walked out the door–slamming it and her heart in one violent action.

Nola leaned against the wall and slowly sank to a crouching position. With the door open, the air froze her. When she heard herself sob, she shut her eyes.

And knew she'd made the biggest mistake of her life.

Nola's hand shook as she reached for a towel partly because the room was freezing since she'd been in the shower so long, mostly because of Del's reaction.

She hadn't seen it coming.

What made her think a proud man, a man so confident, would be excited to learn she'd kept the truth from him? Not only had it been a lie, but also she'd done a lousy job of telling him. It did sound like she'd told him for Mirabella when she really told him because...she loved him.

What did it matter now?

She'd seen the anger in his eyes. The depth ran far too deep for him to be rational. Wrapping the towel around herself, she went to get dressed. Water stains on the carpet glared at her. How like the stains on her heart–all caused by Del.

She'd certainly learned her lesson.

He'd convinced her to leave the safe haven of Soledad, the place she'd finally learned to feel secure in, and now her world shattered much like the shower door could have.

Twice she'd left the protection she'd surrounded herself with–twice her heart was broken.

"I'll never leave Soledad again."

Nola woke the next morning and looked at her clock. Noon. No great surprise. The drive back from Cloudbluff took twice as long since it was during the night—and she cried most of the way home. Now she just wanted to stay in bed—for the rest of her life.

The baby kicked. She had a responsibility to her child. Even if she wanted to go back to sleep, her baby needed nourishment and nausea had returned. Hopefully it was because her stomach was so empty.

Pushing herself up, she reached to grab her robe then looked down. No need since she'd slept in her cloths. When she got up, the room swayed. She grabbed the bed frame, walked to the bathroom and caught her reflection in the mirror.

"So this is what telling the truth, trusting someone has made you look like." Red puffy eyes glared back at her. "Never again, Nola. You'll never again let someone break you like this." Tears ran down her cheeks. Déjà vu.

At the age of seven she'd shed these same tears only then it had been in the bathroom mirror in the Social Services office.

Minutes after her mother's parting words.

The only other person she'd loved and who broke her heart, too.

She grabbed onto the sink and sucked in a breath. Well she was no longer a child. She had a wonderful life here and a baby on the way. She couldn't stand here bawling about how life kept kicking her in the teeth.

Maybe Holly and Del were right. She'd let her past affect her far too much. She would get through this, have a healthy baby, and make a wonderful single mother. After all, she knew the benefits of learning from someone else's mistakes.

No way would she be like her mother or grandmother for that matter. She'd do just fine.

With that, she headed off for a bowl of cream of mushroom soup.

In the kitchen, she bent to get the soup. Her hand froze on the cabinet door when she looked at the neatly stacked cans, all the same kind. She thought of Del. It seemed so long ago that she'd taken him to the grocery store for his first time.

What had she been thinking in telling him about the baby? Her motives seemed noble, but if she'd had the time to think about it, she would have realized the consequences.

Gripping the counter, she wondered what he would do now.

Del rested his head in the palms of his hand, elbows on the desk in his living room. Shaking his head, he looked up. He was going to be a father. Nola's lie had even destroyed the excitement of learning the wonderful news.

He pressed the zero on the keyboard and hoped Henri was not far.

Sunlight highlighted the gardens outside the palace as Henri's face appeared. Thank goodness he had his monitor watch on. Then again, Henri was the most reliable person Del had ever met.

He could see the hesitation on Henri's face. His trusted friend was anxious to know how Del had taken the news. Then again, Henri knew him so well, that look had to be more of what would happen now.

"Your Highness." Henri bowed via satellite.

"Henri, how are things with my father?"

"Much better than yesterday."

Del noticed Henri's eyes darken, his face redden. "Yesterday?"

"*Mademoiselle* did not tell you she spoke to him?"

Del sprang forward. Good thing Henri was merely a screen or he wouldn't have trusted himself not to grab the man's lapels. "Tell me what? Father is all right? What the hell was <u>she</u> doing talking to him?"

Henri hesitated. "*Mademoiselle* inadvertently turned on the screen and King Leon was in the office–"

"Where were you?"

Henri cleared his throat. "The lavatory. He slipped away–"

"Can't you do your job? My father's safety is utmost important–" Del pulled back, ran a hand through his hair. "What is wrong with me, Henri? I apologize."

"Forgive my candor, Your Highness. You are in love."

Del watched the leaves of the grapevines dance about in the breeze behind Henri. Shutting his eyes, he could inhale the fruity scent, feel the warmth of the Mediterranean–and wished that he were home where he belonged. "That is no longer a concern–"

"She told you."

Del nodded. "Only too late."

"It seems, but, Your Highness, she must have had a good

151

reason...to wait."

"What reason could a mother have to keep a child from its father?"

"I cannot say, yet I know *Mademoiselle* Nola is a good woman, a strong woman who cares about you."

"I cannot forgive this."

Henri remained silent for several minutes. "You know your heart."

Del rubbed his eyes. "I thought I did."

"Then perhaps, Your Highness, you need a bit of time to think–to let things clear."

"You've never given me wrong advice before, Henri. For that I am grateful. Yet, she lied to me–a sin I cannot forgive."

Henri grew serious. The screen flickered. Obviously he had no comeback for that one. "I know. Perhaps, though, if you learn her reason, and it is a noble one, you may find it in your heart–" He looked around secretly.

"Henri? Is father all right?"

"He is safe in his favorite spot in the vineyard."

He must have lifted his watch. King Leon came into view, sitting amongst the trellises of grapes, sleeping peacefully. His white hair danced about in the gentle breeze. Del hadn't noticed, but his father had grown thinner, fragile in appearance. Odd that he hadn't noticed until not seeing him for a few weeks. Or maybe he didn't want to see a strapping king failing. Del felt a tug at his heart. A tear ran down his cheek.

Maybe time really does distort memories.

"Thank you for your help, Henri. Is there anything else?"

"Yes, Your Highness," Henri leaned near the watch and whispered. "The reports are in." His eyes took on a glassy stare. "Dr. Desidue has confirmed–"

"Alzheimer's."

"*Oui.*"

Del allowed himself a moment of sorrow. That was all he could afford. He reminded himself that his private life could not come first. A country depended on him. Again, he wished he were born a commoner.

Sitting forward, he shifted into business mode. "Arrange a meeting with the cartel via satellite for tonight. I will hurry the deal along. Fax me the necessary papers after our lawyers firm them up. We can buy ourselves some time if I plan it carefully."

"Begging your pardon, Your Highness. I cannot be certain, but Prince Damien suspects, perhaps in fact–knows."

Del froze. "I don't have to tell you what this means."

"Your coronation must take place immediately or your brother will reign Mirabella."

Because I do not legally have an heir, he thought.

As the radio played music from the big band era, Nola cleaned up the dishes and planned to take a long nap even though she'd only gotten up. Emotional exhaustion was so physically exhausting. Thank goodness it was the weekend. She had nothing to worry about missing–except the man she loved.

The doorbell rang, startling her. She looked in the side of the toaster and groaned. Well, maybe her appearance would scare away whoever it was, and she could take that nap. She looked out of the peephole to see Del standing there.

Oh geez! He didn't look in a very good mood.

If her darned radio hadn't been on, she'd pretend she wasn't home.

"Open the door, Nola."

She jumped back at the sound. This is not good, she thought. He was still calling her by her real name. She reached to at least fix the nest of hair on the top of her head and paused. What the heck for?

Opening the door, she stepped aside. Del blew in like a hurricane. "Can I get you anything?" she asked.

"I didn't come to socialize." He carried a briefcase, which in itself was an ominous sign. They had no work to do since it was Saturday.

"Fine. What do you want? I'm tired."

"That makes two of us who didn't sleep last night."

"Please, Del. I really don't want to argue."

His eyes softened. She'd never want to use her condition as a sign of weakness, but she did feel weak right now. Collapsing onto her couch, she repeated, "What do you want?"

"*My* child."

Nola had never fainted in her life. She did get a concussion as a child in gym one time. The memory of the world growing black came vividly to her as his words hit her. The room started to dim. "No," she said quietly when she wanted to scream. She felt as if she were looking at herself, sitting on her couch, appearing a wreck, and hearing that he wanted to take away her baby.

She never should have trusted him.

He walked near. "Are you all right?" Before she could pull away, he lifted her wrist to check her pulse. "Nola? Do you need a doctor?"

"No." She shut her eyes as if that would energize her. He wanted her baby. He wanted her baby. Energy built slowly, simmered as she repeated the mantra in her head. She looked up to see the worry in his eyes, but his words rung in her ears. Looking away, she pushed up and stood. "No way in hell." She forced herself to look back, to confront him.

His stare grew deadly. "Don't make this harder—"

"Harder than what? You trying to take my child? How much harder could it get?"

"You are prepared to fight me?"

She laughed. Not that it was funny, merely ironic. "I don't have the means, the resources or probably the crafty knowledge to beat you. What I do have is a mother's desire—to fight like hell to keep her child."

"Stop saying the child is only yours. Because, Nola, I will fight you, too. I will gain custody." He slammed his fist against the wall. "By God, Nola, I will have the child kidnapped if I have to!"

"You wouldn't dare!"

He softened. "No, I wouldn't."

She looked away. At least he was honest—something she hadn't been. The emotions pulling at her insides were enough to make her lose her soup. He did have a right to the baby. She knew she couldn't abandon her child as her mother had. Yet, every child deserved two parents, a happy family.

What did her poor child face?

"I know the baby is yours, too, but that doesn't mean I'm willing

154

to give you custody–" She stood taller and caught a glimpse of herself in the mirror behind the couch. Wrinkles covered her blouse and skirt. For a second, she thought of how the silken material floated to the floor last night.

There was no denying how she really felt about Del.

Yet, his demands certainly killed those feelings. "Maybe...we can work out some kind of arrangement. You can at least visit–"

He clenched his jaw. "I do not want to *visit* my child."

"What exactly do you want?" She realized in all the emotion that he hadn't said that he wanted the baby because he loved it. Those words might help her decide what was best.

"As I said, my child."

She'd never been a gambler but this one time she decided to take a chance. "You only want the baby because her or she is your ticket to succession."

Oh God, if she could only take back the words.

A glassy stare filled Del's eyes. She stepped back, expecting him to breathe fire at her. Anger had to have him nearly out of control, yet he stood a statue, the stupid big band music filling the air.

"Del, I'm sorry. It was hurtful of me to say that you only want the baby because of your father's rule."

He looked at her.

"I know that was an unfair thing to say. I...know you better than that. Besides, you could have other children–with someone else–" God, her throat nearly closed forcing those words out. "You don't need our baby to be king."

He paused for what seemed like hours. She watched him, marveling at his composure. It had always amazed her how celebrities could hold up under pressure. She'd been too young to see Jacqueline Kennedy at the late President's funeral, but she'd seen newsreels of it many times. The woman was amazing. Even children held up under extreme pressure like the royal children in England when their mother was taken from them.

Her child's mother wouldn't be taken away from him or her. She'd never allow that.

"I do want the baby. I will love it, *chéri*."

The word sent her flying into his arms.

Del hesitated before reaching up and touching her hair. Gently he patted her head, ran his hand down the side, pushing the strands from her eyes. Inside an emptiness filled his heart, his soul. "If you marry me, *chéri*, all will be solved."

With that, he shut his eyes–and prayed for forgiveness.

Chapter Thirteen

Nola let Del wrap his arms around her. She needed him right now, she admitted. He'd dropped a bomb and at least he was there for the fallout. It wasn't as if he hadn't pursued her and mentioned marriage since their affair in Mirabella.

This time it was different.

He was offering her the chance to be a family–something she never had–a real father. One who loved her child. Now her baby would have its father. Not a long distance one, or one who Nola had forced herself to fall in love with. Falling for Del hadn't taken an ounce of energy. Having to admit it, well, that was another story. She'd held back for so long, it was difficult to let herself believe her true feelings.

There was still Damien's threat, too.

If she told Del about his brother's interference she could possibly cause a rift in what already seemed a rocky relationship. She had no right to do that nor would she want to. Family was too important. Someone who never had a real one, knew that all too well.

"I don't know, Del–"

He leaned down, silencing her with his kiss. If she let him continue, she'd never be able to think straight. Holly was right. The man was magical.

"You know our child deserves what is best. And I would be a good father."

That's what she thought about Rusty. Only this time, she knew in her heart that this man would also be a good husband.

Love convinced her of that.

"How would we– Where would we live?"

"We would do whatever you wanted. We could travel between two homes. I know how important your friends are to you. You cannot stay here all your life with our child, *chéri*. It wouldn't be fair to the baby."

She sucked in a breath, but it did no good. Tears flooded from her eyes despite how hard she'd tried not to cry. It felt good, though, to let them out as it had last night. Her heart needed to heal, and it seemed tears were the salve she needed.

"*Chéri*, I didn't intend to make you sad. I'd hoped my question would be one of joy." He kissed her lips, wiped the tears from her cheeks. "You know how I feel about you."

"I think—"

"No need to think." He chuckled, his chest vibrating against hers. Wrapping her tighter against him, he said, "I love you, *chéri*. I do. Please let me feel...my baby."

Her heart twisted. Gently she placed his hand on her abdomen, and willed their child to be awake. Del leaned near, talking softly. Within seconds, a thud poked at her abdomen.

"Ah!" His laughter brought tears of joy to her eyes. These kinds of tears she welcomed. "*Chéri*, do you have a picture—"

She laughed. "Wait a minute." She reached for her purse and pulled out the sonogram photo Dr. Goodman had given her a month ago. "This isn't real clear. Actually, the baby was so tiny and doesn't even look like a baby yet."

He took it from her hand as if she held a priceless diamond. Tears swelled in his eyes. He looked up. "I'm going to be a father."

She nodded and smiled. "Yes, you are."

"Just a minute." Still holding the photo as if glass, he punched the zero on his watch.

"Your Highness?" Henri asked as he materialized.

Del's hands shook so, Nola helped him hold the photo so he could aim the tiny camera on his watch toward it. "Henri, this is my child."

Nola laughed. "I am not certain you'll be able to see—" She'd never heard a large man blubber so. Henri wiped a fine linen handkerchief across his eyes.

"Is father—"

Before Del could finish, King Leon replaced Henri on the screen. "Father, this is a sonogram, a picture of my child."

"I know what a sonogram is, Delmar. You are going to be a father? I'm very pleased. My, he is going to make a fine king someday." He sniffled amid his laughter.

Nola found herself joining in, knowing she'd made the right decision telling Del. She looked into his eyes as he held the watch in place and whispered, "Yes."

"I shall call you back, Father, Henri." He took her into his arms and held her a shoulder's length away, looking down at her with eyebrows raised. "Yes? Yes means?"

"I will marry you."

"Thank you." He looked upset as he said, "I'm sorry I did not bring a ring. We shall go to a jewelers tomorrow."

"That's all right." Nola leaned into Del. "Thank you" wasn't exactly what she wanted to hear, but she figured he had to be as emotionally spent as she. Reaching out, she touched her finger to his lips. "If this were a movie, we'd be celebrating by making wild love."

He laughed. "As they say, 'roll 'em.'"

She whacked his chest. "I'd love to, but truthfully I don't have the energy. I'm leaning toward a nap right now."

Del took her by the hand. "We need to take care of you. Which way?"

She pointed toward her bedroom, thinking how wonderful to have someone to take care of her.

To her that was a foreign concept.

He led her to the bed, lifted the cover and when she collapsed onto it, he tucked the sheet over her. Then he walked around and slid into the other side. "There is great comfort in merely holding the one you love." He wrapped his arm around her.

She jumped up. Del's eyes widened. "I never told you that I loved *you!*"

He laughed, grabbed her and with a kiss that had them collapsing onto the bed, she nestled into his arm.

A perfect fit.

Del leaned back with Nola tucked safely in his hold. Now he could concentrate on the cartel. His trip here was a success. He had to do the same for his country, and that could only happen when the biggest business deal of his country's existence went through.

Nola slept peacefully while he leaned back and shut his eyes. He couldn't sleep, he knew that. But he'd rest and think. Think of all that lay ahead.

The impending birth of his child.

Damien would bear watching until the legalities were completed.

Del eased Nola to the side and pressed the zero on his watch.

Henri materialized as Del lowered the volume.

"Your...Highness. Congratulations."

Seeing Del in bed with Nola, even fully clothed, was most likely too much for poor Henri. "How is father?"

Henri sighed. "He was quite lucid before, then...."

Del bit his lip. "Do keep up your vigilant watch. And Damien?"

"I run into him throughout the day when usually he would be off with Princess Angelica and the queen. It is most unusual that he remains around."

Del sighed. "We know why he does."

"*Oui*. He did not hear of your news though. I know he was not in the palace at the time."

"Good. When my father is awake, I want you to follow him like a shadow. I know you do your best, but I think we are underestimating his craftiness."

"That seems to be true."

"He was...is a brilliant man and even in the confusion of his disease, he manages to avoid you at times."

"I will not let him out of my sight again. You have my word."

"That's all I need."

Del shifted to the side "Oh, Henri. Good news. Nola has agreed to marry me."

"Congratulations, Your Highness. At least that is one detail we need not worry about any longer."

Nola peeked out from one eye.

The weekend progressed in a series of plans. Nola had recovered from her exhaustion with yesterday's nap only to be thrown into planning her wedding. The past few days were a blur. She could barely remember the details of what she and Del talked about, although she'd never forget what they did in Cloudbluff. She smiled to herself.

Still, there was a niggling thought that bothered her. Henri's comment about one lest detail to worry about. He must have meant that Del had planned to marry her all along when he came to stop her wedding.

Least she hoped that was what he'd meant.

160

Holly had come and gone, after Nola sent her packing with her foolish suggestions. No way would she wear another backless gown. She'd decided the wedding would be small. Holly and Rusty would be witnesses. They could go to the courthouse without any fuss. She'd never been a ceremony type woman anyway. Pouring herself a glass of milk, she sat at the kitchen table and thought of how she and Del could go out for a romantic dinner afterwards.

"*Chéri?*"

"In here." Swinging her head around, she leaned toward the toaster. No great beauty, but a heck of a lot better than yesterday when he'd come over.

He walked in, leaned down and kissed her cheek.

"Milk?" she offered with a smile.

He looked as if she were crazy. "I'll pass. But I will take wine if you have any."

She leaned back, sighed, and touched her abdomen. "You have to rub it in. Don't you?"

Del bent over and kissed the slight bulge. "You are a good mother-to-be."

"Yeah. That, Sherlock, is why I eat meat now when I didn't in Mirabella. Wine's in the cabinet above the frig."

"Ah ha!" He turned and grinned. "I'd figured that out already." With a smile, he walked over and took out several bottles, studying the labels. Nola cringed. How embarrassing to serve a prince wine from this century.

A prince.

The thought brought a trickle of fear to her. Damien's words never left her thoughts, although she told herself her love for Del could overcome anything. Surely he would never have come to Soledad to stop her wedding if he were worried about his chance at the throne.

Obviously Damien had lied. That was a very real possibility she told herself since she knew his reputation and how he acted.
Still, she'd never felt anything like royalty. This was going to be a stretch. Del leaned over, kissed her. "A quarter for your thoughts."

She slapped at his arm. "I told you it was penny."

He leaned over and kissed her again. She reached to touch his cheek. "A future queen can afford more than a penny."

Nola's hand froze. Would she ever get used to the idea that Magnolia St. Clair might someday be a queen? Well, it'd be years before she had to worry about that. King Leon wasn't that old.

"*Chéri*? What took the sparkle from your eyes."

She looked at him, deciding that she'd never lie to him again. "I...it is hard for me to think about being a princess, much less a queen."

"I'm sure. Being born into it, I've never given it a thought."

She pulled her hand back and stood. "You know, Del, I chose to live in Soledad and, okay, I have secluded myself here. It is safe. When I moved here and started working, I felt as if I finally belonged somewhere. Rusty, Holly, and I made a pack as kids that we'd live in the same area. At the time, we were living in a foster home run by Miss Josie in a small Louisiana town."

Del came closer, took a sip of wine, and set his glass on the table. She forced a smile and rested her head on his shoulder. He wrapped her in his hold. Maybe his strength could help her forget. After all, he hadn't abandoned her after she'd lied to him. "Not long after that, they were both adopted into different families. I teased them that Rusty wowed the social worker into putting his name on the top of the list with his charming antics, and Holly somehow finagled an adoption out of it with her craftiness. I even became engaged at the ripe old age of sixteen to get out of foster care. Thank goodness the jerk never showed up at the courthouse. All the while I knew Holly and Rusty were plain lucky–and I never was."

"Your luck is changing, *chéri*. Let it."

"Holly always said I was my own worse enemy, but hurt feelings run deep. It's so much easier to say, do this or do that than it is to actually do it." She looked up to see him wipe his finger across her eyes. "I never cried after my mother left me–now I'm a regular broken faucet."

He laughed. "Before long you'll have no reason for tears. Let today be the first day of your new life. Soon we will wed. Oh, by the way, Henri with his infinite organizational skills has made all the arrangements–"

"For *our* wedding?" She pushed away from him.

"*Oui.*"

"You mean 'yes.' This isn't Mirabella."

"Yes then. The wedding will be in two weeks–"

"What? But that's not enough time. I mean–"

Del hesitated. She could see something in his eyes, but she wasn't certain if it was fear or sadness. "Why wait, Nola?"

He used her real name again. "It's just that...planning takes a long time."

"I told you Henri will handle everything. He has scores of people to help."

"I don't know why the rush."

Del looked at her. "The baby–"

"Well, I guess." But she really didn't see the need for hurrying. "Maybe if we wait a few months–"

"No!" He took her by the shoulders and softened his words. "No. I don't want to wait a moment longer than necessary."

"Okay." But I'll never be able to pull this off, she thought. "Henri will help me?"

"Of course. Henri is quite reliable. He has already sent out press releases–"

"Press? There will be press, newspaper people and television crews, at our wedding?"

"You know that I am a prince. You also know that one day I will be king. Yes, the world likes to know these things. Besides, it is for our country's best interest to keep on best terms with the press. Look what they did to the poor princess in England."

Nola gasped. "You don't mean they'd follow me around? Hound me like that?"

"Don't worry, *chéri*. That's what bodyguards are for. They keep the press–"

"Bodyguards?"

He leaned against the counter. One might assume by his casual stance that he were an ordinary, albeit, handsome, swarthy man. But he wasn't. No amount of pretending he was would change a thing.

Had she jumped into this marriage deal too soon–agreed out of haste? It started to feel as if she had. And there was so little time. It seemed as if Del were rushing her. Having Henri plan her wedding was too farfetched an idea for someone like her to get used to. What would trying to get used to the royal lifestyle be like?

"I guess I'm so accustomed to all of this that it comes as second nature. When you grow up with it–"

"Our child. Our baby is going to be hounded by paparazzi."

"That is what the bodyguards are for, *chéri*." He came near, took her into his arms. "Nothing in this world is going to hurt you or the baby. You must trust me. I will see to it."

She believed him. But her insides clenched tighter than the muscles of his arms holding her tightly. How much control did he or any damn bodyguard really have? England had their share of problems with the press. Not to mention all the movie stars. Geez, how could Nola St. Clair even be thinking of celebrities and herself all in one thought?

"Del, I'm not certain I can do this."

He loosened his hold to look at her. "You will do fine. All brides are beautiful and do fine."

"I'm...not talking about the actual wedding, although that has me scared to death. All those people."

He'd tried to be tender, comforting, but she could see his patience starting to wane. "What are you so frightened of?"

She blew out a breath. "You really can't understand how I feel."

"I am trying, Nola."

Oh boy. There it was again. "Maybe you are, or maybe you'll never understand because of who you are."

He shook his head, grabbed the wineglass and took a long sip. When he set it down, the clink of glass on the counter was the only sound in the room. Well, maybe the thudding of her heart against her chest could be added to the list.

"What is that supposed to mean?" he asked.

She walked across the room and stood behind the chair, leaning on the back. Maybe it was like hiding from him, from the reality of what she faced. "I mean, as you said, you were born into royalty. I've had a tough upbringing and...well, marrying into the Dupre family is difficult for me to fathom."

His anger turned to hurt. "I thought you loved me, Nola."

"I do." She wanted to run and hold him, but knew any contact

164

with him, any inhaling of his scent would cloud her thoughts, and she'd never be able to finish this discussion. "I really do love you, Del. But I have to admit that I don't love the idea of marrying royalty."

"One thing you do not understand, Nola. I *am* royalty. It is a part of me. I cannot change that ever–even if I wanted to. And believe me there were times I wanted to."

Fear gripped her inside. She couldn't even blame the feeling on the baby's kicks. She shook her head. "I'm getting so confused. I want this, yet I don't want to be thrust into becoming a princess–and failing miserably."

His look softened. "Don't you think I've already thought of that? Do you think I would have traveled across the world to marry you if I thought you would not make a wonderful princess."

Her eyes widened. "You did?"

He smiled. "Yes, *chéri*, I did." Crossing the room, he pushed the chair aside, took hold of her, and kissed her forehead.

"That makes me feel a little better, but not any less scared."

"Let me help ease those fears." With that, he covered her lips with his. He'd put all his energy into the kiss while his arms wrapped her so tightly, she almost flinched. Oh, it was wonderful, these feelings of love streaming through her, and she'd never been held, been kissed like this before.

Maybe it was because her hormones where whacked out of normalcy by being pregnant. Or, she admitted, maybe it was because of Del–his royalty, his being so used to getting what he wanted, or because he'd finally tightened the net so she couldn't get away.

Or maybe it was because she'd finally found true love.

Despite his words, she still had her doubts though. "I'll try to let you help, but I don't know how you can get me not to worry that I'm going to ruin your–" Oh geez! If she said "life" she'd have to explain about Damien. How clearly she could hear his words, "You will ruin him."

Del paused and gave her a questioning look. "Ruin my what?"

Only moments ago she'd vowed never to lie to him. Her heart twisted, her thoughts jumbled. She took in a breath to stall for time, and inhaled his scent. Oh great. Now she may never be able to say a coherent sentence.

"What are you afraid of ruining, *chéri?*"

His words came out so tenderly, so caring, she managed to gather her thoughts. She wouldn't lie, but by telling him only part of it, she might get her fears across and still not jeopardize his relationship with Damien. "I'm afraid that you'll never be able to be king if you marry me."

"Why?" One eyebrow rose as he looked at her.

She hesitated. This wasn't easy. Her hand shook as she touched at his cheek. "I'm a commoner. Not the run of the mill commoner either with my past. What will the people of Mirabella think? The press will have a field day with my past. The Mirabellans might hate me—"

He grabbed her with such force, her muscles tensed. "Don't ever say that. Henri knows how to take care of the snooping press. He will play on the empathy of the people. We will reveal the truth before tabloids fabricate stories about you. *Chéri*, no one could hate you."

Her own mother wasn't too thrilled with her. Still, she'd made a damn good life, was a competent nurse, and a very good friend. Proud to have overcome her mother's actions, Nola relaxed in Del's hold. "I only meant as far as not being born into royalty. What if the king and queen don't want you to marry me? Have you even thought of that?"

Del hesitated. He couldn't care less what Queen Francine thought, but his father was another matter. He'd never go against his father's wishes, but in his heart, Del knew his father would approve of Nola. "They and the people of my country will love you."

"But what of the fact that I'm not royalty?"

"I see no amount of talking is going to convince you. So, I must prove it to you, *chéri*." He leaned down and looked at her.

Her eyes widened. She swallowed as if expecting him to tell her it was all off. Reaching down, he took her by the arm. "Come on."

"Where?"

"Do you trust me, *chéri*? Really trust me?"

"It hasn't been easy for me to trust anyone. I'm sure you can imagine why. But, yes, Del, I'm trying real hard, and I want to trust you."

"Good." He led her toward the door.

"Do I need my purse?"

"We're just going to my place."

When he shut the door and watched her walk ahead of him, he prayed that his plan would ease here fears forever.

Chapter Fourteen

Nola walked into Del's apartment and paused. Funny, she'd be marrying him soon, but it felt strange to be here. Maybe she feared why he brought here her. Definitely she was confused about it.

Black leather couches lined the wall with a huge glass entertainment unit on one side. She wasn't surprised to see all the technology, but she was surprised to see how "normal" the place looked. What did she expect? Gold, silk and gaudy brocade to be his choice of décor? Okay, he was a prince, but a modern one, she reminded herself.

The royal residence in Mirabella was more like a French chateau than an ostentatious palace she remembered. She shook her head and sat on the couch while Del busied himself opening one of the cabinets.

"Can I get you something first, *chéri*? Something to drink?"

"You've got me too anxious to swallow a drop. What are you looking for?"

He chuckled. "Give me a second. I don't normally travel with all this–" He pulled out a handsome red leather box. "–but, I confess. Henri insisted I may need it here." He set the box on the glass coffee table with a thud.

"Henri? That man must be worth his weight in gold."

"That he is." He opened the top and lifted a stack of papers.

Fascinated, and still apprehensive, Nola watched his every move. What was in the papers that could help her? He shoved them to the side. Obviously nothing. He looked into the box, sat back, then shut his eyes. She sat forward, felt her forehead wrinkle. "Del," she said softly, "are you all right?"

"Please give me a moment."

She sat back and waited. It had to be the longest moment on record. He opened his eyes. Sadness filled them. The urge to jump up to comfort him had her grab onto a pillow and hold it tightly. She busied herself with taking slow deep breaths. With his confusing look and the way she felt, she needed to remind herself to breathe.

He looked back into the box and reached in, lifting out a beige and gold trimmed book. It looked like a very expensive photo album. What would that have to do with easing her fears or ruining his

169

chance at being king?

"This belonged to my mother," he whispered.

"Belongs," she automatically corrected.

He looked at her and gave a weak smile. "No, *chéri*, this time my English tense is correct. Belonged."

Without a thought, she said, "Actually, it still belongs to the queen–"

"The queen that owned this scrapbook is deceased."

"But Queen Francine–"

"Is my step-mother." He stood, came near and set the scrapbook on her lap. "It is not too heavy?"

She smiled. "No. I had no idea. I mean...what happened to your mother?" Del paused. "Excuse me one moment." He walked to the shelf, took a crystal goblet from the tray and poured himself a drink of wine from what had to be a Wedgwood decanter. Not that she'd ever seen Wedgwood before. "You sure I can't get you something?"

"No. Go ahead," she said, guessing the wine in that decanter didn't come from any grocery store.

After he took a sip, he sat down next to her. "My mother was Queen Clarice. She passed away from leukemia when I was a child. Seven years old, *chéri*. As you were when–"

"My mother abandoned me. I'm sorry, Del."

He nodded. "Mother was sick for so long, it was a blessing she no longer had to suffer. Father took it quite hard and was pressured by the National Council to remarry. Queen Francine came from royalty, *chéri*, and you see what kind of woman she is."

Nola didn't want to say anything bad about his stepmother, but she surmised that he had some of the same opinions. "I still don't get your point."

He opened the scrapbook to reveal of beautiful woman, with eyes as deep as midnight and hair of total darkness. Del looked exactly like her. Only where she was beautiful, he was handsome. "Read this."

It wasn't easy to get her eyes to focus with the way her heart gave a nervous flutter and the aged newspaper clipping he pointed to had faded in time. She leaned near and started to read.

"Out loud, please."

She looked at him then back at the page. "Clarice Gansecky to wed His Royal Highness Leon Dupre–"

"My maternal grandfather was a farmer."

"What?"

"Yes. It is true."

She glared at him. "I don't understand, Del." She gently closed the scrapbook and set it on the table before standing. "I thought you were going to make me feel better. Now I'm more confused about everything."

"Everything?" He got up and held her.

She looked into his eyes. Security filled her, warmed her heart. No longer did she feel trapped in a net. "Everything except about my love for you."

"That's what I needed to hear. My mother was not royalty–and she made a wonderful queen. You can read all about the awards, the tributes to her in the book. Once she made a trip to the United States and saw Andy Williams in concert"

"The 'Days of Wine and Roses.'"

He nodded. "She used to hum it quiet often when I was a child. The press loved her, and they were always kind to her. When she died, father remarried when Damien and I were twelve–out of haste, father later admitted. The press soon learned that the new queen was nothing like my mother. Damien, I'm afraid, bonded all to well with Queen Francine. They are both takers, rather selfish people. However, I do love my brother despite his actions."

Good thing she hadn't said anything bad about Damien.

He smiled. "Feel better now?"

"Yes." She kissed his cheek. "Tell me about your mother."

Nola snuggled on the couch in Del's embrace while he told stories of a queen who spend her days raising money for charity. She traveled but never left her sons with nannies. They went with her until the age of schooling when they spent time with private tutors to be with her. She'd been a ballerina, he said, and gave up her career for the love of Prince Leon. When his father died in a plane crash, she became an instant queen. They'd met when the prince traveled to Russia, and Clarice had been performing with a company in St. Petersburg.

Tears filled both their eyes as he spoke of his wonderful childhood with loving parents until her death. "When mother died, and father remarried, Queen Francine let it be known that she didn't like children. Damien somehow caught her fancy with his...disruptive behavior. She all but ignored me on a daily basis. Father was too busy to notice, and I was too proud to tell him. It hurt deeply."

She kissed him, hugging him tighter. Del's revaluation had her thoughts drift to her childhood and the similarities of them losing their mothers. He certainly had let go of his past. She knew now she had to do the same in order to be the kind of loving mother Queen Clarice obviously had been. If she ever had to face becoming queen, she'd study all she could get her hands on about Queen Clarice.

With a deep sigh, she made up a prayer that she wouldn't have to face that anytime soon.

The days proceeding the wedding ceremony progressed like a dream. Nola became glued to the monitor screen to discuss every detail with Henri each night after work. The man was a genius and even had good taste–except for the table decorations.

She couldn't up and leave her job without giving notice, so she agreed to stay for another week to train her replacement. Del, too, had to finish his last inservices and now had left Soledad to continue at the other hospitals.

She leaned back from the monitor after saying goodbye to Henri and sighed. As exhausting as all this was, it was certainly exciting, too. Holly had been green when Nola told her of the wedding plans. She especially liked the idea of one hundred doves being released into the sky to signify unending happiness for the happy couple.

Holly's face turned a deeper shade of green at the mention of over five hundred guests attending. Then she'd given Nola the biggest hug and whispered that she couldn't be happier. Nola knew that and was thrilled that Ann let Holly take two weeks of vacation on such short notice. Del was flying Holly, Rusty, and everyone else Nola had invited to the wedding in Mirabella on his private jet.

What a sobering thought. She looked at the calendar. Only days to go.

The baby kicked. "Soon, sweetie. Soon you'll have your daddy—"

The monitor crackled. Hopefully Henri wasn't coming back on to argue more about decorating the tables with magnolias. He had the misguided idea that it would be appropriate because of her floral name. She thought she'd made it perfectly clear that she hated the idea, yet the man did have a natural persistence.

Damien materialized.

Nola jumped back. At times he looked so much like Del it was scary—until she looked into his eyes. "Hello, Damien. Del is not here."

"I understand congratulations are in order—on two accounts."

Nola felt a twinge of disappointment. Henri didn't seem the type to gossip, but how else would Damien have known. The screen gave her a sense of security so she asked, "Henri told you?"

Damien laughed. "The man is a steel trap, and my brother the only one who holds the key. I, on the other hand, am a master of lurking. I've heard many a conversation on this monitor because of it."

She shuddered. How much had he heard? "Well, I have a lot to do, Damien. Goodbye."

He leaned near. "Not so fast, Ms. St. Clair."

She should just shut off the screen but no sense in angering her future brother-in-law. She shuddered at the thought. "Did you want something?"

"I want a lot—and do my best to get it." He took a sip of something.

It didn't take her nursing degree to figure out he'd already had far too much to drink of whatever it was. "Maybe we should talk when I get to Mirabella."

He grinned. "You won't want to come to Mirabella, Ms. St. Clair, when you hear what I—" His speech slurred so she couldn't understand the rest. "So, *adieu*—"

"Wait!" She should let him go. Forget what he was trying to say. But she couldn't. "I didn't hear what you said."

He laughed. "Or maybe you don't want to hear it. Hear the truth about your lover—your fiancé," he spit out.

"There is nothing bad you could say about Del that I would believe, Damien." God, she hoped there wasn't.

"Then there is no need for me to repeat myself." He drank more.

"Get it over with, Damien. Obviously you had a goal to reach in talking to me, spit it out."

He lifted the bottle as if in a toast. "Spit it out? Are you sure you can take it–"

"I'm a big girl."

"And getting bigger." He laughed. "You, of course, must know why your fiancé is in such a rush to marry you?"

Her breath held. Rush? Del really had been rushing her. She'd gotten that feeling a few times but let it pass as her active imagination and his excuse about the baby.

"Come on, Ms. St. Clair. A marriage cannot be based on lies. No. No. Why my Princess Angelica and I vowed to be truthful forever." He gave a snide laugh. "Faithful is another story."

"I have no doubt."

He laughed. "My father was to be crowned king a week before his marriage, too."

"A week?" How she wished that hadn't come out so softly.

"Yep. Met my mother and he fell in love like a storybook romance. Isn't that sweet?"

"I already know all that–" Except Del failed to mention that it was only in week that his mother became queen.

"So my darling brother has been truthful to you about some things."

"All things." Suddenly he'd made her doubt if that was correct. "Besides, it must have been wonderful for your father and mother. He must have really loved her and she him–"

"Just like you two. Huh?"

"I love your brother. Yes."

"But does he love you, Ms. St. Clair? Or is your having his kid more the reason? Or, wait, I know–" He took a loud sip. "The laws of Mirabella say that a prince can marry whomever he wishes, even a commoner, *Nola*, but the king is bound to some archaic law. It says the king must marry royalty. So, your darling fiancé will be out of luck if your nuptials fall through."

"That doesn't apply to us—"

Damien laughed then leaned very near. The hairs on the back of her neck rose. "Oh, but it does. My old man is a nutcase. Alzheimer has eaten away at his brain. He's incompetent to find his way to the dinning room much less run a country. Your darling Del is to be crowned in two weeks–a week after he marries the woman carrying his kid. A week after he can marry a commoner while he's a prince. Get my drift, Ms. St. Clair?"

He leaned very near. She could almost feel his breath as he said, "You do understand he is marrying you to get the throne–to beat me out of it. Your pregnancy came in the nick of time. But I'm sure my *honest* brother has already told you all of this."

The screen blurred. Nola raised her hand to her head. This pounding couldn't be good for the baby. She had to take deep breaths or else pass out. She looked to see Damien glaring at her. With a sharp shove of her finger on the switch, he perished.

Much like her life right now.

Chapter Fifteen

Del knocked on the door for what had to be the tenth time. Worry had him about to go find the superintendent–or break the damned thing down. Nola was supposed to be home making wedding plans when he came back from his business trip. Last night on the phone she'd said she would be here now–unless some emergency came up. His heart pounded loudly. He hoped nothing was wrong.

If she lost the baby–he'd....

Yanking his mind to the situation at hand, he knocked one more time. "Nola! Are you–"

The door opened slowly. He pushed it the rest of the way and stopped. No smile covered her face as he'd hoped to see. In fact, her lips were pursed. Her fair skin pale. He could see tension lines across her forehead. Were her eyes a bit swollen? "What is wrong, *chéri?*"

She stepped aside. "Come out of the hallway."

He walked in and shut the door. "You don't look right. Are you feeling– Is the baby all right?" He tried to take her arm, but she pulled away. "There is something going on."

Nola walked across the room and sat on the couch. "Did you have a nice trip?"

He dropped his briefcase onto the table. "Fine. It was fine. My work is all complete."

"That's good." She spoke in a monotone voice and looked as if not seeing him. Perhaps being pregnant was making her feel odd.

"Do you want me to take you to the doctor?"

She turned her gaze to him. "Why are you always trying to take me to the doctor?"

"You seem, I don't know how to explain. But something is bothering you. I'm afraid for the baby."

Looking directly into his eyes, she said, "So your only concern is only for the baby."

"What the hell is that supposed to mean?" He came forward and stood near. "Tell me what you are talking about."

"I'm not one of your lackeys that you can order to do things, Del. I'm still an American citizen and free to do what I want. Henri may jump when you open your mouth, but I don't have to."

"Of course you don't, but you are my child's mother-to-be and if something is going on, I demand to know what it is."

"Demand? Demand?" Yes, he demands and I should follow–a means to an end.

Nola sucked in a deep breath, letting it out very slowly. She had to in order to choose her words carefully. Oh, she wanted to scream at him, accuse him of using her and the baby, and to throw him out on his royal butt.

But the words wouldn't come.

It was so hard to believe all that Damien had said even though it made perfect sense. Del's eyes held a look of confusion along with concern. But was it only for the baby's health? She needed to know that, have him make it clear before she could go on.

"You *demand*?" she repeated, using every ounce of energy keep in control and have it come out quietly.

"Yes, I do." He sat down and took her by the shoulders. His actions were very gentle–not like someone who didn't care about her. "You have me quite worried. If I said or did something to upset you. First I apologize. Second, please tell me what it is, so I can clear up the misunderstanding."

"I wouldn't call your marrying me a misunderstanding."

He looked genuinely confused. "Neither would I when I love you more than life itself. There is no misunderstanding as far as I am concerned."

She hesitated. Since talking to Damien, she'd run this conversation over and over in her head. It was nowhere near as hard to think it–as it was to say it. Besides, damn it, Del was getting her confused. He looked too real, too concerned, and too much in love to be the conniving man Damien had suggested.

Was she letting her fear of trusting a man cloud her thoughts because her own father had never claimed her as his? Because she'd never had a man care for her like Del, and she wasn't certain she could believe his sincerity?

Had Damien only planted a seed of mistrust with her words to twist her thoughts? To break her and Del up?

Del tightened his hold but remained gentle. "I am confused–and frightened."

She looked him in the eye. "What would happen if we didn't

marry?"

He pulled back as if she'd shot him. With a wounded look, he said, "I would sooner die, *chéri*."

She paused. His damn accent, his dark eyes, his magical words made this so much harder. "I want concrete answers. If I changed my mind, what would happen as far as your country was concerned? Not, your emotional state."

He sighed, let her go and stood. "I don't know where this is going, but I would remain a prince and continue at my duties."

"And the throne?"

He glared at her. "What about it?"

"Who would succeed your father?"

"Leave my father out of this."

She noted protectiveness in his voice so she softened her tone, "I know, Del, that your father is suffering from Alzheimer's Disease. I am sorry about that."

His eyes widened. "How?"

"That doesn't matter right now. What matters is who will replace him–if I don't marry you?"

"Damien."

She sighed. "What would that do to Mirabella?"

Del ran his hand through his hair in an impatient gesture. "This is going nowhere. What difference–"

"What would happen? What would you do to prevent your brother from succeeding to the throne."

Del froze. His eyes suddenly held a look as if he understood her foolishness. "I would do *everything* in my power to stop him."

Nola gasped.

"Yes, even marry you, Nola."

She couldn't believe her ears. Damien *had* been right!

And her heart was breaking.

Del walked toward her. "Yes, I would hurry our wedding along so that Damien doesn't have a chance to be crowned before me. I would produce the verified documents to the National Council proving that I was expecting an heir before him. I'm assuming you already know about my father's rule?"

She nodded. "Damien–"

Del cursed. "But, *chéri*, what you don't seem to understand is that this has all worked out so perfectly in my favor. I couldn't have planned it with Henri any better."

"Planned it! My God! You don't have to throw it all in my face. Point out that I am nothing more than a means to and end for you. A mother-to-be carrying a future king. Your...ticket to the throne."

He grabbed her swiftly. Took her lips with a force that both hurt and thrilled. She wanted to push him away, not allow herself to be used, be hurt again. She'd suffered a lifetime of pain and knew she couldn't endure anymore. As fast as he'd grabbed her though, he pulled back. Her hand flew to her lips.

"Don't you see that I meant having the baby and getting married to gain the crown has worked out perfectly, yes, just in time, too. But the reason it is so perfect and wonderful is–because I love you. The rest of that is all 'icing on the top.'"

"Cake," she corrected. "You would love me without any of that–without my being pregnant or your father being ill? You'd still want to marry me?"

Obviously annoyed, Del shook his head. "I know I can't *demand* you do anything but allow me this one time–and for the rest of my days I'll never demand another thing from you. Will you do that?"

She nodded.

"I demand you listen and think very carefully about what I am going to say." He led her to the couch and eased her down. Taking a deep breath, he blew it out and said, "When I came to stop your wedding, I had no idea you were pregnant. Correct?"

"Yes, but–"

"Ah! I demanded you *listen* only."

She bit her lip.

"Fine. So, back to that day when I had planned so carefully to arrive in time to stop you from making a mistake. From me loosing you. Henri and I did plan it all, very calculatingly I might add. I started the minute my private investigator found out that you were to marry Rusty."

"Why you!"

He silenced her with a look. "Yes, I planned to get there just in time to stop you–because I love you!"

180

She flinched. "You don't have to shout–"

He clucked his tongue. "Anyway, I didn't know of the baby, my father was still very much the reigning king. Oh, there were occasional signs of his failing but I–" He wiped at his eye, Nola's heart twisted. "Never guessed that it would happen so fast. Do you understand now that what Damien said is true, but I didn't *plan* any of it. I came to bring you back as my wife–everything else was gravy."

"Ann was right. She said my assignment with you was gravy."

Del's laugh filled the room as he lifted her off the couch and into his arms. "Do we have everything settled?"

"Um."

"No more doubts."

"None."

"Damien has broken up several of my relationships with his lies so that he could become king. But this time, true love cannot be interfered with. No more listening to my brother's lies?"

She shook her head.

"Because this can all be verified by Henri."

"No need."

"Then next Saturday, you will become this prince's bride?"

"Yes. Yes." She grabbed him around the neck and screamed, "Yes!"

"Good, because when we get to Mirabella, I'm going to tell Henri that you called him a 'lackey.'"

She punched his chest.

Nola rushed down the hall of the palace so she wouldn't be late for this special day. She'd lived here for months and still got lost. If she ran into Henri, he'd have her hide. True to his word, Del had told Henri about her calling him a "lackey" hours before their wedding, and now the man teased her unmercifully about her sense of direction inside the spacious palace.

She loved it.

He was the father she never had.

Their relationship was never based on queen and assistant. She loved him and despite his stiff upper lip. She knew he felt the same.

She had the utmost respect for him, but wasn't opposed to making him turn a lovely shade of crimson.

She looked up to see the grand hallway ahead. "Yes!" When the guard opened the gigantic wooden doors, she stepped inside. All heads turned. "I'll never get used to this," she murmured, held her head high and walked proudly to the rear of the room.

Del stood waiting for her. He'd worn his uniform today, looking more handsome than she'd ever imagined her husband could look. Of course, as a new father he beamed from ear to ear at the very thought of having a healthy son.

"Sorry. I couldn't find–"

He shook his head, smiling. "Damien sends his regards. Seems he is too busy in his new position in our factory in Japan to have made the trip."

She punched his arm. "You're terrible. Banishing your own brother to the other side of the world like that, even if he deserved it. But...I do love you."

So far she'd kept her vow never to lie to her husband. Looking at him, getting ready for the ceremony, she made up a prayer of thanks for how well things had turned out. The second their son was born, she admitted to herself and Del that she really didn't want just any father for her baby–she wanted the real thing. Thanks to her little doll, she now had a husband and two families. Leaving Soledad had opened her eyes to the world, and healed her heart. And since, she'd traveled throughout Europe without a hint of a panic attack.

"Oh, *chéri*, the cartel has signed the final papers this morning," Del said, leaning near.

"That's so great." At first she hadn't been sure if she had enough room in her heart to fit the love for her husband, her child and the pride for the king who had taken his country to a new height, but it seemed her heart grew larger each day. Thousands had better jobs, housing and a dynamite childcare center because of Del.

As he led her down the aisle, she smiled to all that turned to watch and gave an extra wide smile toward the press as their flashes lighted the great hall. She looked at her husband and whispered, "This isn't so hard."

He stifled a laugh.

When they reached the gigantic chairs on the dais, he held out a white-gloved hand out to her. "*Chéri.*"

"Thanks." She looked at the guards standing to their sides as if frozen in time. "Thank you that is."

Del grinned and folded his hand over her arm. Leaning near, he inhaled and whispered, "The perfumery in France has done and excellent job of creating your fragrance, *chéri.*"

Whoa. She couldn't have the lusty thoughts that his comment had caused in front of this crowd and her baby. She managed, "Thanks to you."

"Do you think he'll sleep through?" Del asked.

They looked at their son, sleeping like an angle in the lacy covered bassinet in front of them. "I sure hope so. I'd hate to have to nurse him in this crowd." She looked at the hundreds of guests and delegates to the National Council.

Del groaned. Life would never be dull with his queen, he thought, then smiled.

The archbishop leaned forward. "Shall we begin, Your Royal Highness?"

Del nodded.

Nola grasped tightly onto his arm. She'd made it through their gigantic royal wedding months ago, what seemed like hundreds of royal functions in between, but this royal baptism was a whole new ball of wax.

And she wasn't afraid to admit she was a nervous wreck.

Not only was she a queen, she was a mother. Still, she silenced her fears with a squeeze to her husband's arm, knowing she wasn't in this alone. Her child would have the world, when she herself never even had a home.

"We have gathered today to celebrate the joyous occasion of welcoming, His Highness Prince Leon Francois Philippe Henri Dupre...."

Del looked at her.

"I threw that last one in."

He smiled. "Henri will be thrilled."

"And I'm calling the kid Little Hank."

Del grabbed her arm tighter, or he'd burst out laughing in front of his entire country. He looked up to see the press tucked neatly in the rear of the great room, knowing Nola had once again put them in their places, perfectly. Scanning the room, he looked for Henri. He should be seated in front of them.

At the same time, Nola tugged his arm. "Where is Henri?"

"I don't–"

The giant double doors opened in unison. A red-faced Henri hurried in, pushing a huge television screen down the aisle. Del could see it pained the man to have to interrupt.

"Excuse me, Archbishop. Please wait for a moment," Del said.

Confused, the archbishop looked over his shoulder. "Oh my." His ruddy color had poor Reverend Shaneborn beat by a mile.

Nola and Del looked at each other. "If you start to laugh, I shall have to lock you in the dungeon, *chéri*."

"Hey, I've been doing a damn good job as queen, but this is too much of a coincidence."

"I know." He sighed. "Henri must not know any other way to interrupt a ceremony."

"Well, I for one am glad he did interrupt that first one. But what's going on now?" She looked down the aisle. "What is it, Henri?" she asked to the poor man as he wheeled the screen to the side of the dais.

"Forgive me, Your Royal Highness. But, your father has asked me to set this up so that Queen Nola's American friends could join us. It seems they had trouble connecting."

"Cool!" Del jabbed her in the side. "Okay, I still need work," she whispered. She looked at Del's father seated in the front row and gave him a warm smile.

He nodded, looking very regal. "My gift to you for making me a grandfather," he said in with the clarity of a scholar. His wife looked at the screen and frowned.

A tear stung Nola's eyes. She knew Del's father meant the words, but she also knew in a moment of clarity this was his way of welcoming her into the Dupre family.

She was now accepted.

Holly materialized on the giant screen. "Nol? Oh, my. Can they all see me?"

Del laughed. "Yes. Welcome."

Rusty and all the OR staff called out their greetings. The poor archbishop now looked a wee bit more flustered than Reverend Shaneborn ever did. Holly moved in front of the camera. "Sorry we are late. Guess your American family isn't as technologically adept as the Mirabellans. But we wouldn't miss this for the world!"

Nola wiped at her cheek. Del leaned over and kissed her. She nodded to Del's father and mouthed, "Thank you."

Her husband squeezed her hand and whispered, "Tonight, my queen, we shall give your American friends another reason to visit us—in nine months."